GIDEON DEFOE

THE PIRATES!

In an Adventure with the Romantics

Gide　　　　　　　　　　　　es in
Lond　**The Urbana Free Library**　rates!

In a　To renew: call 217-367-4057　*rates!*

In a　or go to "*urbanafreelibrary.org*"　*n an*
　　and select "Renew/Request Items"
Adventure with Communists, and *The Pirates!*
In an Adventure with Napoleon. You could be
forgiven for thinking he is a bit of a one-trick
pony.

		DATE DUE		~~8/12~~
	~~DEC 03 2012~~			
			~~OCT 25 2012~~	

Books by Gideon Defoe

THE PIRATES!
IN AN ADVENTURE WITH SCIENTISTS

THE PIRATES!
IN AN ADVENTURE WITH AHAB

THE PIRATES!
IN AN ADVENTURE WITH COMMUNISTS

THE PIRATES!
IN AN ADVENTURE WITH NAPOLEON

THE PIRATES!
IN AN ADVENTURE WITH THE ROMANTICS

THE
PIRATES!
In an Adventure with
the Romantics

PIRATES!
In an Adventure with
the Romantics

or

Prometheus versus a Terrible Fungus

Gideon Defoe

VINTAGE BOOKS
A Division of Random House, Inc.
New York

Library of Congress Cataloging-in-Publication Data
Defoe, Gideon.
The pirates! in an adventure with the Romantics, or
Prometheus versus a terrible fungus / by Gideon Defoe.
p. cm.
ISBN 978-0-345-80290-3
1. Pirates—Fiction. 2. Romanticism—Fiction.
3. Authors, English—19th century—Fiction. I. Title.
II. Title: Prometheus versus a terrible fungus.
PR6104.E525P65 2012
823'.92—dc23
2012023748

To Peter Lord,
Who has his own film studio. You can't
compete with that, can you, Sophie?

CONTENTS

LIST OF ILLUSTRATIONS

'Fig 1: The Bering Land Bridge at the last glacial maximum, as reconstructed from the latest research. Fig 2: Vin Diesel in "The Pacifier".'
72

'Sparklechops leapt over the fence. "Go Pony, go!" shouted Putin.'
85

'Eliza burst into tears. The world's biggest parsnip – and it was ruined!'
91

'If the President's button phobia ever got out, Brigid knew she could kiss goodbye to that promotion. She squeezed the trigger.'
122

'Meringue!' said Illiana.
131

One

FATE WORE A
TENTACLE

'The most exciting way to start an adventure,' said the albino pirate, 'would be to open in the sinister lair of the International Crime League, eavesdropping as they plotted their most audacious crime yet – the theft of the Queen's brain!'

'That's ridiculous,' said the pirate with gout. 'The most exciting way to start an adventure would be to wake up inside a room, next to a dead body, two pieces of coal, and an unexplained carrot – but there's apparently *no way in or out of the room!*'

'How about finding yourself in a regular-looking café . . . but then, when you open the door – it turns out you're *in space!*'

'What if, overnight, plants started walking *backwards.*'

Soon all the pirate crew joined in the argument about what the most exciting way to start an adventure might be. Usually this would escalate from polite to heated to vociferous before you could

3

say 'guts everywhere', 'arterial spray' or 'horrific splatter pattern', but today, because the pirates were sitting in the vestibule of a fusty Swiss bank and one of the bank clerks was giving them a stern look, they decided it was probably best to keep the noise down. The albino pirate stopped waggling his cutlass at the pirate with bedroom eyes and stared at a pot plant instead. The pirate with gout picked up a magazine and went back to reading an article about dividends. The pirate with a scarf gazed out of the window to where the pirate boat lay parked on the rain-drenched, achingly dull shore of Lake Geneva, thought a bit about the nature of irony, and yawned.

Inside the bank manager's office the Pirate Captain tipped back in his chair, swung his boots onto the big mahogany desk and did his most winning smile, which involved showing off all of his teeth, even the molars.[1] His years at sea had left him tanned

---

[1] Although 'Thou shalt not lean back on thy chair on two legs' did not make the Ten Commandments, the first recorded injury caused by this reckless chair practice is in the Bible (Samuel, Chapter 4, Verse 18). Eli the priest fell backwards off

and weathered — but weathered in a good way, like an antique globe or a vintage fireplace, not in a bad way, like Val Kilmer or a mouldy coffee cup — and if you were to compare him to a type of gastropod, which was the latest thing his crew tended to compare him to, he'd probably be a luxuriantly bearded conch, or maybe a whelk with a pleasant, open face. The Captain wasn't keen on being compared to types of gastropod, so he'd been trying to persuade them to compare him to other things instead:

Type of thing the Captain would prefer to be compared to other than gastropods.	If he was one of those things he would be either a . . .	Or a . . .	Reasons he felt this was an appropriate thing to compare him to.
Greek God	Zeus	Poseidon	Air of authority. Inspires great works of art. Looks good naked.
Ocean	Pacific	Atlantic	General brininess. Changeable moods. Sometimes contains fish.
Fine wine	Château Lafite	Prosecco	Surprisingly bubbly. Goes well with grilled lamb.
Natural Disaster	Mudslide	Infestation of Killer Bees	Sweeps all in his path. Arrives unexpectedly. Easy to draw.

his seat and broke his neck when he got some bad news about the Ark of the Covenant.

He hadn't had much luck so far. The crew were adamant that he had a lot more in common with whelks. The Captain pointed out that unlike whelks – which use a large muscular foot to pin down their lobster prey – he had *two* large muscular feet, didn't care for shellfish as much as people made out, and lacked any kind of extendable proboscis tipped with a sharp radula at all, but once the pirates had something in their heads it was hard to shake it.

'So, I was thinking that a thousand doubloons should do the trick,' said the Captain, pointedly not scratching his shell, because he wasn't much like a whelk. 'I realise that sounds like quite a lot, but you know how day-to-day expenses can mount up. As it happens, I made a list, in case you don't.' He pulled a napkin from his coat pocket. 'Let's see: Spare bits of rope – thirty-five doubloons. Press-ganging – that's fifty. New hats – that's another fifty.' The Captain tapped his tricorn. 'Might seem frivolous to you, but it's important to keep up with the latest season's fashions in order to maintain the lads' respect. You can't put a value on respect. Where was I? Ah, yes: Christmas presents for Scurvy Jake, twenty-five . . . new barbecue . . . forty . . . and the rest is "sundries".'

The bank manager, who like most people in his income bracket was made mostly of jowls, peered over his half-moon spectacles. 'Eight hundred doubloons for "sundries"?'

'Can't get by without the sundries. Say the word a few times, it's very satisfying. "Sundries".'

'Pirate Captain. In today's wintry financial climate, credit is not so readily available as it once was.'

'Ah, no, of course. The *markets*,' said the Pirate Captain, with a conspiratorial nod. He had recently taken to dropping phrases like 'the markets' into conversation to give the impression he understood economic matters. The bank manager pulled a face as sober as his suit.

'And your account is now nine thousand doubloons in the red.'

'Is red the good colour? I can never remember.'

'No, Captain. Red is not the good colour.

7

We've been trying to contact you for several months regarding this matter, but you don't appear to have replied to any of our letters.'

'Ah. If you think I was avoiding them, then you're wrong. I actually didn't even *open* those letters because I assumed they were birthday cards. And, thanks to a clerical error, you thought I had a birthday twice a month.' The Captain helped himself to a complimentary mint from the little tray on the manager's desk, and did his winning grin again. 'I'm doing my winning grin again,' he explained. 'I don't know whether you've noticed, but if you look closely you'll see I've had tiny grinning faces carved into some of my gold teeth to make it an even more winning grin than it would otherwise be.[2] So. How about this loan, then?'

---

2 Aztec women used to stain their teeth bright red with the crushed bodies of cochineal beetles, to make themselves more sexually appealing. Until recently modern women could achieve the same effect using crushed mauve Smarties, which contained carmine or E120, a food colouring derived from the same type of beetle. Unfortunately this was recently replaced with a dye extracted from red cabbage, which is not so sexy.

'Sorry, Pirate Captain,' said the bank manager. 'I'm afraid that this time, we really won't be able to oblige.'

The Captain puffed out his hairy cheeks and tried another tack.

'Look, you have to understand – piracy isn't like other jobs. One minute you're swimming in pearls and eating diamonds instead of cereal, the next you're clinging to a raft made from dead pygmies without a penny to your name. The thing we're dealing with here is what I believe your sort refer to as "a temporary liquidity issue".'

'I'm well aware of the piracy business model,' said the bank manager, wobbling his jowls sympathetically. 'After all, we pride ourselves on being the bank of choice for . . . the more unsavoury professions.' He gestured at the wall, which was covered in pictures of famous pirates, gangsters, deposed dictators and other bank managers.

'It just doesn't seem like piracy is a very lucrative career for *you*, Pirate Captain. Have you considered doing something else? I hear

9

plumbing is surprisingly well paid. People will always need plumbers.'

The Pirate Captain leapt to his feet as if he'd found a jellyfish in his boot. 'You insult me, sir! I am a pirate to the core! If you cut me in half – this is a metaphor by the way, so don't actually do it – if you cut me in half you wouldn't find intestines and bits of spine and blood. No! It would be more like a stick of seaside rock and running through that rock would be the words "ONE HUNDRED PER CENT PIRATE" in big bold letters.[3] I'd never give up the pirating life! Never!'

'I heard you were a beekeeper for a while.'

The Captain sat back down. 'That was different. And, anyway, it turns out there's no money in bees either. People aren't ready for my avant-garde take on honey.'

The bank manager tapped a pencil on his desk and adopted the conciliatory tone that works well with toddlers when they've been told they can't eat glue.

---

3 At one time or another, Michael Barrymore, Sandi Toksvig and Matthew Kelly have all had their names immortalised in specially made sticks of rock.

'Shall we talk about repayment terms?'

'Sorry. I'm afraid you've got my blood up now, and I find it impossible to think about money when I'm having an emotion. I demand to see my lawyer!'

'This really isn't a legal matter, Pirate Captain.'

The Pirate Captain tossed his beard about and waved his arms. 'Oh, it's all becoming clear to me! Shall I tell you what the problem is? It's that you don't know what it is to *live* and *laugh* and *love* and run a man through! You've never tasted the salty air on your tongue or waved heartily at a mermaid! It would be impolite to call you a shrivelled little bean counter who wouldn't know drama if it kissed you on the mouth, but nonetheless – I'm afraid that's exactly what you are. You people have no flair, no romance, no sense of adventure! Everything's just numbers for you! Well, you can't reduce *passion* and *flair* and *eating ham* to numbers, sir! Good day to you!'

And with that he swept out of the room, slamming the door behind him. The bank manager shook his head and made a weary note in his ledger. A few moments later the door creaked open and the Pirate Captain crept back in, picked up a handful of the complimentary mints and crept back out again.

'Right lads,' said the Pirate Captain, tapping his cutlass against his boot buckle to get everyone's attention. 'There's no way to sugar-coat this – we're going to have to tighten our belts.'

The pirate crew, now sprawled on the deck of the pirate boat, made a few unhappy noises, and some of the more literal-minded ones sucked in their bellies and wondered out loud if the bits of seaweed that held up their stripy trousers counted as belts.

'Let's be honest,' the Captain continued. 'It was pretty much 100 per cent me and my care-free attitude to finances that got us into this mess, so arguably I've already done my bit. Therefore it seems only right that these unfortu-nate economies should fall squarely on the rest of you. Probably sensible to start with the elderly and disabled pirates,' he waved cheerily at the pirate with a hook for a hand and the pirate with skin the texture of old accordions, 'seeing as they're less able to stand up for themselves.'

The pirates all nodded at this logic, because it seemed pretty watertight.

'With that in mind, I've decided to ring-fence the budget for my beard-care products, and it goes without saying that I'm not going to be eating any less ham than I usually do. But everything else is on the table. So: who's got any ideas?'

This wasn't the first time the pirates had found themselves in a tricky financial position, so they ran through a few of their usual moneymaking schemes. The pirate in green thought they should start a mania for tulip bulbs; the pirate with long legs thought they should try their hands at counterfeiting pigs; and Jennifer, the former Victorian lady who had joined the crew on a previous adventure, suggested that they could ask children for their pocket money in return for running through any siblings they didn't get along with, because children were quite immoral. Several pirates had heard that 'white collar' crime was a pretty easy option, but they didn't really know what it involved. Also very few of them wore collars of any description, and those that did certainly didn't have *white* collars, partly because nothing was very clean onboard the pirate boat, and partly because they knew not to wear white after Labour Day. They were pirates, not animals.

The Captain listened to everyone's pitches and clicked his tongue thoughtfully.

'They're interesting suggestions,' he said, 'and I'm glad to see that some of you are finally learning to think outside of the box. But you know me: the only thing I prefer to *following the path of least resistance* is *failing to consider the long-term repercussions of my actions*. So I thought we might start by selling off some assets, because selling off assets doesn't really require much planning or intellectual effort at all. It so happens that I've already taken the liberty of getting the pirate with a scarf to draw up a list.'

The Captain signalled his trustworthy number two, who stepped forward, cleared his throat and began to read.

'Assets: two cabin boys, condition poor; one barrel of weevils,[4] six months past their best-before date; an old seal carcass; a particularly large barnacle that looks a bit like a face; some moss.'

The Pirate Captain clapped his hands together. 'Well, that's a promising start. Very promising indeed. Pirate in green, run down to the news-agent's and pick up a copy of the *Geneva Gazette*. Somebody is bound to want fantastic assets like those.'

---

4   Numbering over 50,000 distinct types, the weevil family contains more species than any other group of organisms. The longest weevil is the Giraffe Weevil, which grows up to 80mm (0.044 per cent of a pirate) in length.

It wasn't as ridiculous a plan as it sounded, because back in those days people still bought newspapers, and soon all the crew were sat round the desk in the Captain's cabin poring through the 'Items Wanted' section. Not having a girl-friend meant that the Captain never did much tidying up, so the cabin was the familiar jumble of nautical paraphernalia, olden-days bric-a-brac, and mementoes from past adventures. There was a fake nose from their adventure with spies, a wax Viking from their adventure at the Jorvik centre, and a genuine letter signed by Abraham Lincoln from their adventure at an autograph fair.

'Anybody found anything yet?' he asked, turn-ing over another fruitless page of newsprint.

'Sorry, Pirate Captain,' said Jennifer. 'People seem to want prams, second-hand cuckoo clocks, open-minded partners for fun times in the countryside, but very few are looking for a large barnacle or a barrel of weevils.'

The Captain scanned through a couple more pages of adverts himself, his heart sinking fast, like a lazy shark. He was just about to set fire to the newspaper and throw it at a cabin boy, when he spotted the very last advert, in florid type near the bottom of the page.[5]

WANTED!

Exotic Adventure! Should contain romantic elements, mild peril, and foreign travel. A lively denouement involving a murder and/or a mysterious woman with flashing eyes would be regarded as a bonus. Good price paid. Apply to the Villa Diodati, Lake Geneva

---

'Those are all exactly the kind of elements *our* adventures tend to include!' exclaimed the Pirate Captain, drawing a ring around the advert and holding it up for everybody to see. Those pirates who could read murmured excitedly. The pirate in red frowned.

'Doesn't it seem like it might be a little demeaning? Hiring ourselves out like that? We're not circus monkeys.'

---

5 The first newspaper advertisement was placed in 1704, seeking a buyer for an Oyster Bay in Long Island. Contrary to popular belief, pearl oysters produce pearls by covering an invading parasite, not as a result of ingesting a grain of sand. Australian astronomers estimate that there are ten times more visible stars in the universe than grains of sand on the planet.

'And more's the pity,' snorted the Pirate Captain, with a rueful shake of his head. 'If I had a crew of circus monkeys I wouldn't be in these financial straits, would I? I'd be a leading theatrical impresario, happily knitting you waistcoats for our next sell-out show, "The Captain and His Mischievous Capuchin Crew". It would be adorable, whilst at the same time containing a serious message about the peaceful coexistence of species.'

He banged his desk to show that his mind was made up and that any further discussion would be futile. The Captain often thought that if he hadn't become a pirate, or an architect, his third choice of profession would have been a judge, because he really did enjoy banging things to make a point.

'Jump to it, you swabs – new plan! I want you all looking as exotic and perilous as possible. That means scars at their most livid and stumps at their most unsightly. Hoist the jib, loosen the bowsprit, all that nautical palaver. For today . . .' He paused and held his cutlass aloft. It felt like an important moment and that he needed to

finish his sentence with something both stir-
ring and memorable, yet at the same time pithy.
'. . . we respond to a newspaper advertisement,'
said the Pirate Captain, who wasn't great at
thinking on his feet.

Two

THE BOAT THAT
BLED BLOOD

'Are you sure this is the right address?' The Pirate Captain peered through the letter-box and tried pulling the bell-rope again.

'Villa Diodati,' the pirate with a scarf said with a shrug. 'That's what it says on the gate.'

'You don't think some other coves beat us to it, do you, number two? Neptune's lips! I hope it wasn't those confounded cowboys, peddling their idiotic Stetson- and cactus-based adventures.'

He gave the rope a final desultory yank, sighed, and turned to face the crew, who were neatly lined up in the driveway, dressed in all their most extravagant outfits, trying their best to look employable. 'Well, lads, sorry to get your hopes up, but it seems like this is a bust. Probably time we drew lots to see which one of you I sell to the paste factory first.'

But before any lots could be drawn or any pirate bones could be melted down into a delicious paste, the door suddenly swung open, and a flustered young woman popped her head out.

'Hello?' she said, brushing a curl of brown hair from her face. 'Can I help you?'

The Captain looked at the woman and narrowed his eyes. She had cheekbones and skin and nice teeth in all the right places and proportions, and if years at sea had taught him anything, it was to be suspicious of attractive girls, in case they turned out to be sirens trying to lure him to a watery grave.

'Well?' said the woman, cocking her head.

'Excuse me just one moment,' said the Pirate Captain, stepping back and taking his deputy to one side. 'What do you think, number two?'

'Think?' repeated the pirate with a scarf, a bit confused. The Captain's thought processes could be a little difficult to follow.

'The girl! Do you suppose she's . . .' his voice dropped to a whisper. 'You know: an oceanic seductress, here to feast on my briny soul?'

'A siren?'

'Well, it occurs to me that even sirens proba-bly have to move with the times, so perhaps placing a newspaper advertisement is the nowadays equivalent of luring sailor-folk with their enchanting song.'[6]

'Hello,' said the young woman, with a wave. 'I *can* hear you. And no, I'm not a siren.'

'Exactly what sirens tend to say of course,' the Captain noted with an apologetic frown.

'Yes. I imagine it would be. Look, I'm terribly sorry, but now isn't really a great time—'

A tremendous crashing noise interrupted her. It was instantly followed by the sort of bellowing that, two hundred years later, would be most readily associated with Brian Blessed.

'Not again,' said the woman, rolling her eyes, which, the Captain noted, were exactly the right

---

6 The Starbucks logo is probably today's most famous siren. She is a double-tailed 'baubo siren', or a 'cross between a mermaid and a Sheila-na-gig'. The etching from which the first logo was copied had a big unsightly belly button, but this was removed from the design on the assumption that people didn't want to look at big belly buttons whilst drinking their morning coffee. Subsequently Starbucks have also covered up her breasts and obscured her split tail, which was felt to be too sexually suggestive. Though if you find yourself getting aroused by old Starbucks' logos because you can see *too much fish tail* there are issues you need to address.

shade of hazel, and rolled about her eye sockets in a really pleasing way. She disappeared back inside the villa, leaving the door ajar. The pirates followed, because they were pirates and so not really attuned to social etiquette.

Inside the villa there was a lot of tasteful lubber furniture and a whole deal more banging and bellowing going on. At the top of a spiral staircase a pale and serious-looking young man hammered at a door, whilst from the other side muffled curses and the occasional roaring wail drifted out onto the landing.

'What on earth is he *doing* in there?' cried the woman, bounding up the stairs towards her companion.

'I'm afraid,' said the pale young man, 'that he's having one of his bleak tempestuous moods.'

'Oh, good grief. What's it about *this* time?'

'I'm not sure. Everything was fine a moment ago: he was wagering that he could swallow an entire Toblerone in one gulp, which I contended to be impossible, because of that particular confectionery's awkward shape. Then he said that triangles and nougat were no match for the tempests that rage in a man's soul, and stomped up here. He bellowed something about ending it all, and now he's locked himself in.'

The woman hammered at the door again. 'Byron? Can you hear me? This is ludicrous! Please come out.'

The Pirate Captain had almost never encountered a situation where he didn't fancy himself the best man for the job despite the lack of any evidence to suggest that he was.[7] This being no exception, he strode across the hallway and started up the

---

7 The Pirate Captain is exhibiting the Dunning-Kruger effect, a cognitive bias in which unskilled people make poor decisions, but their incompetence denies them the metacognitive ability to appreciate their mistakes. The unskilled rate their ability much higher than it really is, whilst the highly skilled underrate their own abilities. Actual competence may weaken self-confidence, as competent individuals assume others have an equivalent level of understanding.

staircase, hoping that any onlookers would notice how he took the steps three at a time.

'Spot of trouble?' he said, flashing the woman a grin that was a slightly different shape to his earlier 'winning grin' because this one was meant to convey 'devil-may-care confidence'. 'Not to worry, attractive brunette; and whoever you happen to be,' he nodded vaguely at the pale man. 'I think I might be of assistance.'

'Who on earth are *you*?' said the man, looking the Captain up and down in surprise.

'I'm the Pirate Captain,' the Pirate Captain replied, with a quick flourish of his hat. 'Think Zeus, a bottle of Château Lafite or a mudslide. And these are my pirate crew,' he pointed at the crew who were dutifully following up the stairs behind him. 'This is my loyal, though somewhat dull, deputy, the pirate with a scarf. That's the albino pirate, who's probably best described as the boat's happy idiot. That's the pirate in green, he's sort of an everyman type. The pirate in red is the surly one. The rest are pretty interchangeable. I wouldn't bother trying to keep track of them if I were you. Oh, and this is Jennifer, a genuine lady who we met on an earlier adventure in London.' The Captain suddenly pulled a knowledgeable face and nodded at the door. 'So. Delicate business. But as luck would have it, I'm something of an expert at emotionally charged situations such as these. Brace yourselves.'

He took off his coat and started to roll up his sleeves. The pirate with a scarf tapped him on the shoulder. 'Are you *sure* you're an expert at emotionally charged situations, Pirate Captain?' he asked quietly. 'You're not just thinking about the time you tried to talk Little Jim out of killing himself? When he jumped to his gruesome death, even though he'd only gone up the mast to clean the crow's nest in the first place?'

'That's not how I remember it at all, number two,' said the Captain, one of whose many skills was remembering things differently to how they had happened, which is a useful trick to pick up once you get past the age of thirty. He turned back to the young woman and adopted an authoritative tone of voice. 'Now: when dealing with a potentially unbalanced person contemplating suicide, the important thing is to make sure you have the *element of surprise* on your side. Catch them unawares.'

And with that, before anybody could challenge this piece of psychological reasoning, the Captain charged at the door with a great piratical roar, sending it splintering off its hinges. He careened right through and straight into a bookcase. Manuscripts fluttered about like a lot of papery rectangular seagulls.

Across the room a strapping man with a cascade of wavy black hair so shiny it looked like it had been conditioned in something really expensive, like lobster sweat or dolphin's eggs, balanced on the balustrade of an ornate balcony. The sudden appearance of a pirate didn't appear to bother him at all. He furrowed his brow, and held up two billowy shirts. 'Which one do you think would look best on my shattered, yet still unfeasibly dashing corpse?'

'I like the one with the ruffles,' said the Pirate

Captain, picking himself up off the floor. 'You can't go wrong with a lot of ruffles.'

'Yes! Quite right!'

The man quickly stripped off his shirt and changed into the one with more ruffles. Then he pulled a pistol out from his belt. 'Be a stand-up fellow and pass me that bottle, would you?' He pointed rakishly to the mantelpiece, upon which sat a small green bottle that had the same logo on the side as the pirates had on their flag.[8] The Captain obliged. He was impressed, because *pointing rakishly* isn't an easy thing to pull off. The man attempted to get the top off the bottle, but it was difficult because he already had the pistol in his other hand. Then he tried holding the pistol in his teeth, but the stopper was obviously jammed tight. Eventually he got it out with a pop, but spilt half the poison down his freshly laundered shirt. He cursed a bit.

---

8 In his autobiography, *My Wicked, Wicked Ways*, Errol Flynn claimed that the second most poisonous substance in the world is the human tooth. He knew this because while nude, he punched a Spaniard off his boat, got a tooth lodged in his fist and ended up in a coma for four days.

'I don't want to be rude, but do you maybe think this is *overkill*?' said the Captain, gesturing to the balcony and the gun and the poison.

'No, sir!' said the man. 'It is to be the most spectacular suicide ever witnessed! A truly tortured and poetical end, destined to echo down the ages. I was going to involve a gas stove as well, but there were logistical complications.'

He raised the gun to his head and the bottle to his lips. A fountain burbled in the garden below. 'Right, here goes,' he said, striking a pose so heroic it made several watching pirates, who had piled into the room after their Captain, faint clean away. 'My glorious final act! Goodbye, cruel world!'

'Byron! Stop!' cried the young woman, hurrying towards him.

The Captain remembered why he had gone in there in the first place. 'Excuse me,' he said, putting his hand up.

'Yes?' said the man, pausing on the very edge of the balustrade.

'We all have those bleak sort of days when everything seems hopeless. A monkey's eaten your sextant, some native witchdoctor has sold you a cursed eye-patch, your crew won't shut up about gastropods. But before you go ahead with this, I'd like you to take a moment to think about all the *other* more life-affirming things knocking about the universe.'

'That does sound like it would be fun, but I don't want to miss the light,' the man waved at the sunset. 'It's going to really add to the poignancy of the moment.'

'It won't take long,' said the Captain, pulling another napkin from his pocket. 'I happen to have made a list. I like lists.'

'Oh fine,' said the man. 'Go on then.'

'Right,' said the Captain. He ran through his quicker vocal warm-up exercises and then began to read. 'A list of items I consider to be so miraculous and unexplainable that they make life worth living: Giraffes' necks. Magnets. Lava. Shooting stars. Rainbows. Pelican beaks . . .'

'Goodness,' said the woman, half an hour later. 'It's quite a long list, isn't it?'

'The Captain's very thorough,' agreed the pirate with a scarf.

'. . . that odd neat handwriting psychopaths have. Venn diagrams. Snow globes. Tiny cheeses. And, last but not least, girls in thigh-length boots.' The Pirate Captain stopped, wiped his forehead and gave a bow. 'That's it.'

'You forgot dressing up a sausage dog in a coat shaped like a bun,' said the man.

'It *is* good when people do that,' agreed the albino pirate.

'But you get the gist?' asked the Captain.

'I do.'

'So, faced with all that natural wonder in the world, why are you throwing yourself to your doom?'

'Boredom, sir!' cried the man, waving his arms hopelessly. 'The sheer grim, unremitting tedium of it all! We came to this godforsaken country because, for some unfathomable reason, it has a reputation as the most romantic place in the world. A "heavenly valley", Coleridge said, unmatched by any other.'

'That's the sort of stuff people end up

spouting when they put opium on their crumpets instead of butter,' explained the young woman with a sigh.

'Are you sure this Coleridge chap wasn't just pulling your leg?' asked the Captain. 'I've got a nemesis who's always doing that sort of thing. Well, I say nemesis, but you know, we rub along all right, really. I suppose a more accurate description would be "constant thorn in my side". His name's Black Bellamy. Have you met him?'

The man shook his head sadly. 'No, sir, I have not, but would that I had, for he sounds more interesting than anything Switzerland has to offer. For the entire duration of our stay it has rained, a ceaseless, idiotic drizzle.[9] And in two months – two months! – we have failed to undergo a single spiritual epiphany, have a senses-shattering encounter, or enjoy an unexpected escapade. The closest we've come to anything like

---

9 The poor weather of 1816 – known as 'the year without summer' – was caused by the eruption of Mount Tambora in Indonesia, an explosion so huge it could be heard over a thousand miles away.

that was three weeks ago, when Percy here spotted a cow out of the window that we all agreed had nice eyelashes, and yesterday, when Mary scored fifteen points for the word "Quagmire" whilst we were stuck inside playing yet another game of that infernal Boggle.'

'Well, if that's the only problem then you're in luck,' said the Captain. 'Because, as it so happens, we're here about your recent advertisement.' He held up the newspaper and pointed to where he'd circled the advert.

'Advertisement?' The man looked at him blankly. 'What in the ocean's thundering swell are you talking about?'

'I was under the impression that you were seeking *an exciting adventure?*'

There was a small cough from the other side of the room. Everybody turned to look at the young woman, who blushed.

'Sorry, I should have mentioned that,' she said, with an apologetic smile directed at her companions. 'It just seemed like it might be a good idea. You're not the only one who's been going a bit loopy, B – the thought of having to go on one more alpine jaunt makes me want to eat my own elbows. So a few days ago I took it upon myself to put that advert in the paper. Though to be honest, I'd rather given up hope – so far the only responses have been from people trying to sell us second-hand cuckoo clocks.'

The pale man gave the girl a rather disapproving look, and the wavy-haired man scratched his chin thoughtfully. Then, his impending suicide seemingly forgotten, he roared with delight, and jumped down off the balustrade. 'Why, that's fantastic! Good thinking, Mary! Bright cookie, this girl.' He threw the poison and pistol over his shoulder, because littering wasn't considered antisocial in those days, then crossed the room towards the Pirate Captain and gave him a hearty handshake. 'What did you say your name was again?'

'I'm the Pirate Captain,' said the Pirate Captain.

'I like your neck, Pirate Captain! That's a man's neck! Like an oak!'

'You've got a very impressive neck yourself.'

The man roared again, apparently for no real reason beyond the love of roaring, and smacked his pale friend on the back, making him wince. 'Isn't that brilliant, Percy?' He paused and suddenly looked serious. 'But I'm sorry! Where are our manners? We must introduce ourselves!' He turned and beckoned to the young woman. 'This ravishing beauty is Mary Godwin.' The girl smiled and did a sort of half curtsey, half wave. 'This cloud of tubercular vapours is Percy Shelley.' The young man gave an awkward little bow. 'And I'm George Byron. You may have heard of me, if you happen to subscribe to *Young, Brooding and Doomed*, the quarterly newsletter that details my exploits. We're poets.'

None of the pirates subscribed to *Young, Brooding and Doomed*, because they tended to go for less erudite nautical publications like *Ports Illustrated* and *Teen Scene*, but they did their best to look impressed anyhow.

Byron flopped into a big armchair and lit a cigar. 'So – *adventure*! Not a word to be trifled with. What kind of adventures do you offer?'

'What kind of adventures *don't* we offer might be a simpler question,' replied the

Captain. 'Though actually no, probably asking what kind we offer makes more sense. So far we've had an adventure with a Man-panzee, one with a great white whale, another one with some communists, and one with Napoleon Bonaparte himself. Wall-to-wall action, every one. Sometimes there's even a vague sort of theme. Anyhow, I can provide references if you want.' He got the pirate with a scarf to waggle a pile of references. 'You'll notice that they're all written in different colour pens, so they're definitely genuine. And now, if you'll permit, my crew will perform a medley of pirate things to convince you to hire us.'

As they'd prepared earlier, the crew shuffled forward and started to do a mostly uncoordinated display of stuff that they thought people would associate with pirates. Jennifer did her impression of a sultry Spanish Princess and heaved her bosom whilst pretending to be overcome by the drama of the cutlass fight being staged by the pirate with gout and the pirate with a hook for a hand. The albino pirate said 'avast' in a way that suggested he didn't actually know what it meant. The pirate in green gave a short presentation about the importance of tar. And most of the rest of the crew just walked around in circles because they couldn't think of anything more appropriate.

When they had finished, Byron looked confused, Shelley looked dubious and Mary of course was a woman, so her feelings were impossible to guess.

'As you can see – all the romance and thrills of the High Seas, in one colourful package,' the Captain said, handing out a brochure he'd got some of the more visually creative pirates to knock up that morning. 'You'll find the details in there. You get to stay on an honest-to-goodness pirate boat. There's a guaranteed minimum of two feasts per day. All toiletries and towels will be provided. And there'll be more swashbuckling than you can shake a parrot at. Best of all, it's a special one-time-only bargain price of only a hundred doubloons per adventure.'

'A hundred doubloons,' said Mary, flicking through the brochure. 'That does seem very reasonable.'

'Plus sundries,' said the Captain.

Three

THE SPECTRAL BRINE

'I can't believe we're having an actual feast with actual pirates!' exclaimed Byron, happily thumping the boat's dining table. 'See here – this placemat is in the shape of a treasure map! Brilliant!'

The pirates had spent the afternoon giving their guests a tour of the boat, taking care to point out the important nautical bits, like the sails. The Captain, worried they might be disappointed with how small the place was, ended up walking Byron and his friends around it three times, but in a variety of directions, giving the masts and cannons different names on each circuit. After that he'd got the lads to sing a few of the more risqué shanties, and now they were in the midst of a pirate feast. In honour of their guests being poets, the pirates had laid on a menu of dishes made out of food that rhymed, because they wanted to look classy.

'Of course – being a pirate is not *quite* as

glamorous as people make out,' said the Captain, thinking he could afford to dial it back it a little, having just finished an unlikely story about blowing up the kraken by a kicking a barrel of dynamite at its head. 'There's a surprising amount of paperwork these days. And it turns out there's a lot of boring technical what-have-you that makes the boat go along. You can't just strap a porpoise to the wheel and swan off to have cocktails. Learnt that the hard way.'

'Pfft!' roared Byron, taking a big bite out of his lamb and clam ciabatta. 'I won't hear it! What a life. Not knowing what the next day might bring! Adventuring! Derring-do! Boys wearing outsized jewellery! It's exactly the kind of thing we've been looking for.'

'But you say you're writers? That must be interesting too,' said the Pirate Captain, turning to Mary and waggling his eyebrows at her in as debonair a way as he could. 'As a matter of fact, I'm something of a gentleman of letters myself.'

'Really?' said Mary, incredulous. 'You write? What sort of things do you write about?'

'Oh, you know,' said the Captain, waving his fork in a vague circle and looking to whichever side it is that you look to when you're not being entirely honest. 'Emotions. Waves breaking on a rocky shore. The usual artistic bits and bobs.'

'We're not just "writers",' interjected Shelley, picking unenthusiastically at his spam and yam salad. 'You can't reduce a man to the label of his profession.'

'Look!' said Byron, 'now I'm drinking pirate grog out of a mug made from a skull! It's as atmospheric as it is impractical!'

'So how *would* you describe yourselves?' asked the pirate with a scarf.

'We . . .' said Shelley, flicking his hair with a flourish, '. . . are *romantics*.'

'Ah,' said the Captain, after a long pause, and with what he hoped would pass as a 'wise' nod. 'Is that like a gang?'

Shelley visibly bristled. 'No, Pirate Captain. It is not "like a gang".'

'Are you sure? You do *seem* a lot like a gang. You've obviously got a brave and headstrong leader,' he waved at Byron, who was too busy laughing at a spoon with a mermaid drawn on it to notice, 'a plucky girl,' he indicated Mary, who just arched an eyebrow and went on thoughtfully licking her ham and jam popsicle, 'and a slightly ratty one,' he pointed back at Shelley, who frowned. 'So you're pretty much there. Though you should probably get a loyal dog with a sensitive nose as well. Always find it's best for gangs to have a loyal dog with a sensitive nose. And matching jackets! The jackets could have some romantic emblem on the back. An albatross? They mate for life, you see, so it's one of the most romantic creatures. Though it might look too much like a seagull unless you write the word albatross underneath it. Only then people could think your gang was called "the Albatrosses" rather than "the Romantics". Doesn't have to be an albatross. I'm just brainstorming here.'

'It's not a gang,' Shelley persisted, sounding petulant. 'In fact, we don't approve of *any* sort of organisations. We believe in the individual! It's a whole new way of looking at life.'

'Oh, right, got you,' lied the Captain.

Shelley leaned forward, and his eyes blazed a bit.

'We have a dream, Captain. Imagine, if you will, a world run not by politicians . . . but by artists.'

'That sounds terrible,' blurted out Jennifer, because she was the crew member who tended to say out loud what the rest of the crew was thinking.

The poet didn't appear to have noticed. 'The world has become so drab of late,' he went on. 'Everything's about logic and industry and science and things being "rational". Well, we reject all of that!'

'But surely,' said Jennifer, 'science and "being rational" are quite good? You know. Advances in medicine. Technological innovation. Not being in thrall to mumbo-jumbo superstitions?'

'I'm afraid you have a terribly Western view of culture, young lady. Can science write you a poem? Can medicine paint you a landscape? Can engineering make your spirits soar?' Shelley sat back and looked pleased with himself.

'It can build you a sewer,' pointed out Jennifer. 'I quite like working sewers.' She turned to Byron and Mary. 'You all go along with this romantic stuff, do you?'

Byron shrugged. 'Percy's the theoretical one. I tend to be a bit more . . .' he fished for a description. 'Hands on. Do you know, I once punched a donkey? For no reason at all! Just the simple thrill of living in the moment. If you ask me, the key to a really *artistic* way of life is total impulsiveness. No thinking things through if you can possibly help it.'[10]

'Yes, I'm like that,' said the Captain, offering Mary some zucchini blinis. 'The other week I refused to eat anything that wasn't a suckling pig and/or drizzled in honey. Pure impulse.'

'Exactly! I can see we're cut from the same cloth, you and I. Men who must constantly breathe in all the sensual delights the world has to offer, lest we suffocate without them.' Byron threw out his arms expansively. 'Tell me, Captain, do you ever just find you've spent the entire day marvelling at how nice your own hair is?'

---

10 An almost certainly apocryphal story concerning Lord Byron is that when told it was against regulations to keep a dog in his room at university, he got himself a pet bear instead.

'All the time!'

'Me too!'

'Oh good grief,' muttered the pirate in red, burying his face in a napkin. 'There are *two* of them.'

After the feast, the pirates served coffee and chocolates in the Captain's cabin and refused the Romantics' offers to help wash up, on the grounds that they were paying guests. Because it was the nineteenth century people had to make their own after-dinner entertainments – they couldn't just slump in front of old *Friends* episodes and say, 'Oh, this is the season when Chandler was on crack, look how *thin* he is,' like they do nowadays – so Shelley suggested they play a game.

'It's a little thing we invented whilst stuck in that villa,' he explained. 'We challenge ourselves to come up with the most moving work of literature possible on the spot. You've got to think fast, but it's just fun. Not a competition.'

'Not a competition, right, got you,' said the Pirate Captain. He didn't fancy Shelley's chances much.

'Each person throws out three completely random objects and the other has to improvise something literary about them. The winner is the one who moves the audience to tears.'

'See, that's interesting, because us pirates tend to play a similar sort of game. After dinner, we close our eyes and throw cutlasses around. The winner is the one with as many eyes at the end of the game as he had at the start.' The Captain shrugged. 'But hey! You're paying – so let's give your version a shot.'

'Pirate Captain, as our host, I'd like you to give me my three objects,' boomed Byron.

The Pirate Captain didn't like to be put on the spot. Three objects was a lot of objects and it seemed a bit much to get a question like this out of the blue. But nonetheless he rubbed his temples to get the brain juice flowing and did his best to think. 'A ruined lighthouse!' he said, after a while.

'Don't make it too easy for him,' said Percy.

'An owl's egg.'

The Pirate Captain thought hard about the last one. He'd never played baseball, because baseball didn't really get popular until the 1850s, but if he had, he'd have realised that what he was looking for was a *curveball*.

'A loss adjuster in a medium-sized insurance concern.'

Byron cracked his knuckles, fluffed his blousy shirt and climbed up to stand on the remains of his pudding.

> *'O Egg! Who comes from such wise arse,*
> *That borne thee spinning to scrivener's jaws . . .'*

Byron's poem was quite long. The loss adjuster, Philetaerus, was an arrogant, moody chap, doomed to inspect maritime property damage as penance for the death of his sister. He stalked the coast, haunted by a supernatural owl that may or may not have been the spirit of his monstrous father. The owl mostly taunted him by laying ghostly eggs into his open mouth when he was asleep. The end came when Philetaerus was swept from a ruined lighthouse into the sea by a wave that represented conventional society.

Everybody agreed it was a fantastic work of literature, and if gasps were the measure of success, Byron would have carried the night. But nobody cried. Shelley's lip wobbled, Mary seemed to have drifted off about halfway through, and the crew got bogged down debating whether ghost owls would eat ghost mice or regular mice.

Next up was Shelley. Inspired by the bric-a-brac that littered the Captain's cabin, Byron suggested a happy wolf's head, a plaster mermaid and a pair of scissors.

After each one, Shelley did a small, serious nod.

'A tricky triumvirate, my friend!' he said, 'but not so tricky that it can overcome the Muse. I give you . . . The Waning Lament!'

The Pirate Captain was pretty sure Shelley had some sort of system worked out for his improvised poetry, because there was a clever bit where he rhymed 'lupine grin' with 'marine chin' that definitely sounded rehearsed. Unfortunately, Shelley's verse went over the heads of most of his audience, because despite their many years sailing with the Pirate Captain, none of the crew were able to decipher the clever allegory of a water spirit's desire to cut loose the ties of normal family life and journey to a Fairy Queen's tomb, so once again nobody cried. Shelley looked fed up.

'That was a very good attempt, Percy,' said the Pirate Captain, magnanimously.

'Who's next? Mary?'

Mary seemed about to speak, but Shelley cut in. 'No, Pirate Captain. Mary and I are very forward thinking, and, as such, we feel that it's wrong, politically, for a woman to perform purely for the entertainment of men. Isn't that right, Mary?'

'Oh,' said Mary, wincing a little. 'I suppose we do think that, yes.'

'So it's your turn,' said Shelley, turning back to the Captain. 'What, I wonder, might you make from a dartboard, a burning flame and the concept of free will.'

'Well, that's easy,' said the Pirate Captain, not missing a beat. 'A dartboard and a burning flame were in love, but then the concept of free will came along and the dartboard fancied it, so there was a love triangle. It all came to a head and in a moment of passion the burning flame accidentally set a tiny puppy on fire.'

The pirates looked distraught.

'Sadly, the puppy's injuries were too grave and he passed away. The dartboard and the other things were pretty cut up about it and stopped arguing. The end.'

Everybody apart from Percy clapped. Tears streamed down Byron's big cheeks, and he raised his mug of grog aloft. 'Bravo, Pirate Captain! Bravo! A tragic tale! Such humanity!'

Shelley shifted in his seat. 'I'm not saying it wasn't a nice story. It was very moving. But can I ask one thing?'

'Fire away.'

'How did the dartboard talk?'

'Good question,' said the Pirate Captain, pondering for a moment. 'I'd say he probably had a little mouth in the bullseye. Do you want me to do the voice?'

'No, I think that's all right,' said Shelley, pulling a face and looking rather irritably at his pocket watch. 'So, this evening has been a lot of fun, but if it's not too rude a question, when *exactly* does our exciting adventure begin?'

'Aarrr,' said the Pirate Captain, at something of a loss. 'I'm sure one will be along any moment now.'

The cabin fell quiet. A few rats messed about in the rafters. The boring sound of cowbells wafted across the lake. After a moment, Mary coughed. 'How do they tend to get going? The adventures, I mean?'

'It can be all sorts,' explained the Captain. 'Unexpected octopus attack.[11] Some sort of

---

11   In Hawaiian mythology it is thought that the Octopus is the sole survivor of an earlier, alien universe. In Marvel comics, it is *known* that Galactus is the sole survivor of an earlier universe from before the Big Bang.

nefarious trick played by my aforementioned nemesis, Black Bellamy. Or, I don't know, a flaming seagull might crash through that porthole at any moment, carrying a curious summons in its beak.'[12]

Everybody stared at the porthole for a while. Flaming seagulls pointedly failed to crash through it.

The Pirate Captain grinned awkwardly. 'Oh well, you know what they say – a watched adventure never boils. But, um, feel free to have the run of the boat until whatever exciting thing is going to happen kicks off. There are some very romantic barrels of weevils knocking about, you might want to check those out.'

---

12 Seagulls keep their feathers waterproof with 'preen oil', which oozes from a nipple-like protuberance near the tail. The seagull smears it around with his or her beak.

Four

A FANTASMAGORIA
ATE MY FACE

Early next morning the pirate with a scarf found the Pirate Captain pacing back and forth across his cabin, like a hairy metronome, or a sad polar bear. So far as anybody could tell, they still weren't on an adventure, and the Captain was worried that if a grisly murder or a woman with flashing eyes didn't turn up soon then the Romantics might start to have second thoughts about the entire business. After a little while he stopped pacing, picked up a tin of biscuits and perched on the edge of his desk, looking thoughtful.

'So what do you think of our guests, number two?' he asked his deputy, as he fished around for a custard cream, which were still his favourites.

'They seem nice enough,' the pirate with a scarf replied, sitting down on the Captain's chaise longue. 'Mister Byron is certainly very enthusiastic.'

'Yes – good nautical sort, Byron. Brine in his veins. You can just tell. Not so sure about that Shelley fellow. You know how brilliant I am at working out people's entire personalities solely based upon their physiognomy? As soon as I clapped eyes on him I thought – "Hello! Here's a chap with a suspicious upper lip!" Too fleshy. Or not fleshy enough. One of those.' The Captain paused, then rubbed his beard and ostentatiously stifled what the pirate with a scarf recognised as a 'nonchalant yawn'. 'How about the other one?'

'Mary?'

'Is that her name? I forget.'

'I like her. She seems both clever and curious,' said the pirate with a scarf, after a moment's consideration. He knew that the Captain liked him to keep character descriptions to no more than two easily identifiable traits, because anything more gave him a headache.

'Clever and curious. Hmmm.' The same distracted expression that the Pirate Captain normally got walking past a butcher's crept across his face. 'Did you notice her eyes?'

'I noticed she *had* eyes.'

'Yes, they're sort of like . . . limpid pools. But brown. Can limpid pools be brown?'

'I suppose so. If the limpid pools have mud or gravy or something like that in them,' said the pirate with a scarf.

'And then there's her skin. Her skin's like . . . like . . .'

The Captain floundered for a bit, and the pirate with a scarf thought about suggesting 'satin' or 'fine alabaster', but the Pirate Captain was never going to get any better at doing similes if he helped him out every time, so he held his tongue.

'. . . like bacon!' said the Captain, triumphant. 'Well, shiny like bacon can sometimes be.'

'She's certainly quite striking,' agreed the pirate with a scarf.

'If you say so. Can't say she made much of an impression on me. To be honest, I barely remember anything about her at all.' The Captain trailed off, because, at that moment, through a porthole, he caught sight of Mary emerging from her cabin. She strolled across the deck, draped a

63

delicate hand over the boat's railing, and shook her hair loose in the breeze. For some weird reason the Captain was pretty sure that she managed to do all that in slow motion. He hopped off his desk and patted down his beard.

'Anyhow, number two, can't stay and chinwag all day. I've just realised that I should probably go and carry out my regular boat inspection.'

And, before the pirate with a scarf could point out it was Thursday, and that boat inspections were on Tuesdays, and also that they only took place every six years or so anyway, because the health and safety regime onboard was notoriously lax, the Pirate Captain had already barrelled out the door.

The Captain's boat inspections were always pretty slapdash, because they mainly just involved him looking at the ropes and planks and barnacles and then nodding to show that he approved of whatever they happened to be doing. But today's inspection was even less thorough than usual, because as soon as he was done approving of a blocky wood thing with a hole in it, the Captain forgot all about inspecting things and turned his attention to Mary instead. She didn't seem to have noticed him, as she stood gazing out across the lake with a faraway look on her face. The Pirate Captain cricked his neck, narrowed his eyes, and decided that now seemed a good time to employ his patented conversational gambit, which was also known as 'the standard protocol' – first of all he would establish himself as *aloof*, then he'd be *funny*, and finally he'd be *deep*. It never failed to impress a lady and when it did, that was the exception that proved the rule, because it was foolproof.

Aloof

'Excuse me,' said the Captain, sauntering over to Mary. 'Would you mind moving? You're in the way of some vital nautical equipment there. This is a pirate boat, not a women's changing room in a fashionable boutique.'

Mary looked down at where he was pointing. 'I'm sorry, Pirate Captain. I didn't realise this . . . uh . . . dead crab, is it? . . . was so important.'

The Pirate Captain poked the crab with the toe of his boot. 'Well, you wouldn't, because you're a lubber. As it happens, that dead crab tells us how many sharks there are nearby. I'd explain how, but I'm not sure your vague Romantic brain would be able to handle the science. It's something to do with barometric pressure. For your information, there are no sharks nearby.' He did his nonchalant yawn again. 'So, anyway, what are you doing out here on deck?'

'I was just admiring the view, Pirate Captain.'

'Hmmph! I've got more important things to worry about than *views*,' he snorted. 'Like destiny. I'm quite high-minded and *aloof* from the mundane, you see. You may want to look that word up in the dictionary, because you probably don't know it. I'll save you the trouble – "aloof" means "conspicuously uninvolved and distant". That's me all over.'

Mary seemed a bit put out, which was usually a sign that the standard protocol was working its magic.

'Have I offended you, Pirate Captain? Because I'd say you're being more "obnoxious" than "aloof".'

The Pirate Captain thought he'd probably done enough 'aloof' by now. The trick was making the transition to 'funny' as seamless as possible.

Funny

'Anyhow!' said the Pirate Captain. 'I heard a funny story the other day. There was a pirate and he couldn't remember where he'd buried his treasure. So he press-ganged a classful of children and forced them to dig up an entire island and then – this is the funny bit – then he realised that he'd buried it on a *completely different island*. Ha ha! Imagine!'

'Those poor children. That sounds awful!'

'The *wrong island*. You can picture his face.'

Mary didn't laugh. The Pirate Captain assumed that maybe she didn't understand pirate humour and preferred blander land-based jokes. 'Would it be funnier if he was a cowboy? No? Okay, what do you think of the Duke of Wellington? Imagine if he got his arm stuck in a door. I expect it would sound something like this . . .'

The Pirate Captain did an impression of the Duke of Wellington and then followed it with an impression of Queen Victoria trying to buy a tin of shoe polish and then a sequence of other famous people in situations that you wouldn't expect to find them. Mary somehow continued to manage to keep from laughing. The Pirate Captain decided satire wasn't really her thing, so he changed tack and just pulled a series of funny faces.

'Well, Pirate Captain,' said Mary after a few more awkward minutes had passed, 'this has been . . . very interesting, but I think I should go and check on Percy.'

Deep

The Pirate Captain decided he'd better squeeze in the final stage whilst he still had a chance, so he stopped pulling a funny face and instead pointed at his eyes, which he tried to make look as big and caring as possible.

'No need to run off, Mary. Can I call you Mary? Mary. Why don't we talk about you and any feelings you might be having. I'm a very good listener.'

Mary stifled a laugh, tried to look the Pirate Captain in the eye and then had to look away again. He decided this was probably a delayed reaction left over from 'funny'.

'Let's see now,' she said. 'I can tell you that I'm a feminist. I believe in the right of women to be treated as equal with men.'[13]

The Pirate Captain took off his hat and held it to his breast. 'Neptune's teeth! I don't believe it! I'm a feminist too. I thought I was the only one,

13   Mary's mother, Mary Wollstonecraft, wrote *A Vindication of the Rights of Woman*. Her father, William Godwin, who was a bit better at titles, wrote *Jack and the Beanstalk*.

but there are two of us! Every day I wake up and look out of my porthole at the big sky and think how awful it is that somewhere under that same sky, a woman is being overlooked for promotion or told to "give us a smile" by some builders.'

'There's rather more to it than that, Pirate Captain.'

'Of course there is. You don't need to tell me how hard it is to be a feminist in this cruel manly world. I've suffered more than anyone. You should hear the stick I get from other pirate captains for having Jennifer on board. It's hardly her fault that, as a woman at sea, she brings terrible luck to the whole crew. I really don't blame her for the misfortune she's caused – the bankruptcy, my temporary madness, that business with the cannibal and so on. Because she's more than made up for it with her can-do attitude. So, if you want to do any feminism here on my boat, feel free. And if you get taken with the urge to burn your petticoat, I have a large fireplace in my office.'

'I appreciate the sentiment, Pirate Captain, although I'm not sure you've quite grasped what feminism involves. In fact, you sort of sound as if you have an ulterior motive.'

The Pirate Captain was pretty sure that 'ulterior motive' was just another way of saying 'hidden depths'. He nodded.

'Yes,' he sighed. 'If you knew how many hidden depths I had your pretty eyes would pop right out of your winsome face. Not literally of course – that would be disgusting. I wouldn't envy the man who had to clean up a pair of popped eyes, especially given the state of this deck. I'm not sure we even have any cleaning products that work for popped eyes, although I suppose a general viscera cleaner would do the trick. You'd need some elbow grease and a decent scourer, depending on how long you'd left the eyes there because, between you and me, the lads can be pretty lazy and they've been known to leave organs lying about on deck for weeks, no matter how many times I tell them. Do you Romantics have the same problem?'

Mary shook her head. 'Not really, Pirate Captain.'

The Pirate Captain remembered he'd been

talking about something less interesting but more important. 'I'm sorry, I've gone off on a tangent. What was I saying before I got on to popped eyes?'

'You'd done "aloof" and "funny" and were about halfway through "deep", I think.'

'Oh yes. Anyway, I'm also a quarter Irish, one of the most sensitive ethnic groups.'

It was about now that he'd expect the attractive lady to swoon into his arms, but Mary stayed unexpectedly upright. A creeping realisation started to dawn on him. 'Wait a minute. Did you just say "halfway through 'deep'"?'

Mary gave the Pirate Captain a frank, but not unfriendly, smile. 'I'm afraid so, Pirate Captain. I *have* enjoyed this chat a great deal, but I really think I should go to check on Percy. On account of him being my fiancée.' She held up a finger with a ring on it, rather apologetically. 'See you later, Pirate Captain.' And with that, she turned on a shapely heel and disappeared below decks.

The Captain stomped back into his cabin, and made enough noise banging astrolabes into things to ensure that the pirate with a scarf would come and find out what was going on.

'You're not going to believe this, number two,' he fumed, 'but my patented Aloof/Funny/Deep method has drawn a blank.'

The pirate with a scarf looked sympathetic. 'Sorry to hear that, sir.'

'Possibly I got the ratios muddled. Maybe these Romantics require more of the deep and less of the other bits? Or perhaps she's got the wrong sort of brain, one that somehow fails to respond to my natural magnetic pull. Like a broken compass. Yes, that's probably it: she's like a miserable, creamy-skinned broken compass.'

The Captain slumped into his armchair.

'Also, she says she's engaged to that Shelley fellow. It's preposterous!'

'Ah, well, that does make the situation difficult.'

'I don't see why! Look at me – I'm married to the sea, but I'm not letting that get in the way of things, am I? Besides, we're on a *lake* at the moment, and you know what they say: whilst the big wobbly blue cat is away, the pirate mice will play.'

'Oh well,' said the pirate with a scarf, who found matters of the heart both confusing and slightly frightening. 'Any sign of an impending adventure? I just bumped into Mister Shelley on the way to breakfast, and he seemed rather cross that nothing had got going yet.'

The Captain digested this news, and tapped his teeth. 'You know what the problem is – curse of the intellectual! I've been *over-thinking* it.'

'I suppose that *could* be the case,' said the pirate with a scarf, doubtfully.

'It's time to employ my trademark direct approach. Listen up, number two: here's the plan – we're going to kill two fish with one cannonball. By which I mean metaphorical fish, obviously. One of the better-looking fish is Mary, and one of the fish is getting this adventure started.'

'Is the cannonball metaphorical too? Or is it a regular cannonball?'

'No, the cannonball is a *clever plan*, for which I'm going to need a couple of the crew, the remains of that seal carcass, and for you to run me a bath.'

Five

IN THE GRIP OF
GHOSTLY GUMS

Byron, Shelley and Mary had barely got half-way through their inedible breakfast of muesli and fusilli when a strange unearthly wailing noise echoed down from the deck of the pirate boat. Nobody needed much more of an excuse to put aside their bowls in relief and hurry upstairs to see what was going on.

'Oh! My word!' exclaimed the pirate with a scarf, who was already out on the deck waiting for them. 'Look at this poor creature!'

He pointed, slightly sheepishly, to a greyish lump writhing about near the mast. An eagle-eyed observer may have described it as looking a great deal like the pirate in red wodged into a hollowed-out-and-then-sewn-back-up-again seal carcass.

'A poor seal pup,' the pirate with a scarf continued, apparently unable to meet anyone's gaze, 'cruelly harpooned by Eskimos.' The pirate in green popped up from behind a barrel, waving a harpoon and dressed in an oversized parka.

'Eskimos?'[14] said Shelley, incredulous. 'On Lake Geneva?'

'He must have been washed aboard by a tidal wave.'

'A tidal wave?' said Shelley. 'Again – *on Lake Geneva?*'

The pirate with a scarf pleadingly tried to pull a 'just go with it' sort of face. 'Who might sort out this awful situation?'

At that point the doors to the downstairs of the boat crashed open and right on cue the Pirate Captain bounded out onto the deck, with nothing but a few beads of water to cover his modesty. The Romantics gasped, but none of the pirate crew so much as batted an eyelid, because they were hard-pressed to remember an adventure when the Pirate

---

14 The Inuit word for 'a conical mound of ice' is 'pingu'. The episode of *Pingu* titled 'Little Accidents' was banned due to graphic images of penguin urination. There would probably be a thousand words for 'yellow snow' in Eskimo if Eskimo was a language, which it isn't.

Captain *hadn't* found an excuse to get unexpectedly naked.

'Dear me!' the Captain exclaimed. 'I was caught unawares, just in the midst of a relaxing bath. And what's this? A poor seal pup, cruelly harpooned by Eskimos.'

'I already did that bit,' said the pirate with a scarf.

The Captain rushed forward, punched the Eskimo, and cradled the misbegotten seal in his arms. The seal pup cursed a bit, and mumbled something about stupid plans always involving dressing up as creatures.

'I'm going to have to heroically administer mouth to mouth,' said the Captain gravely, leaning down to where the seal pup appeared to have a scowling second face poking out from the inside of its own mouth. Once the seal spluttered back into life, cursed and flopped around some more, the Captain hoisted it above his head and threw it over the side of the boat.

'There you go! Back to the inky depths from whence you came! Tell your blubbery brethren that they have nothing to fear from those Swiss

Eskimos so long as the Pirate Captain sails the waves.'

He saluted and then turned to his gob-smacked audience.

'Tremendous! That's one of the most noble things I've ever seen!' roared Byron. Shelley groaned. Mary once again seemed to have got an oddly timed fit of the giggles. The Captain beamed at her. 'I'm sorry, Mary,' he said, subtly starting to flex various muscle groups. 'I hope you're not too overcome at the sight of me like this, but as I said, I was just having a bath, and didn't have time to cover my strapping, manly form.'

Eventually Mary managed to forget whatever had been amusing her, and got her composure back.

'Are you feeling okay, Pirate Captain?' she asked.

'Sorry?'

'It's just that you seem to be suffering from some sort of . . . terrible spasms.'

'Devilishly attractive spasms?'

'Not *exactly*.'

The Captain deflated a bit, stopped flexing,[15] and sat down on a barrel.

Shelley looked cross. 'I hope that little episode wasn't supposed to constitute our adventure? Because I have several doubts about the incident's veracity.'

'It wasn't *just* an adventure, I was killing two birds with – oh, never mind,' the Captain trailed off and decided to stare sulkily at the horizon. Everybody hovered awkwardly. A few of the crew did their best to melt into the background. Again, not literally, because that would be horrific.

'Goodness me,' said Mary, after a while, just to break the tension. 'You certainly have a lot of tattoos, Pirate Captain.'[16]

---

15 The finale of a bodybuilding competition is the 'posedown', when competitors line up and run through a series of muscle poses simultaneously. There are two approaches to winning at a posedown – you should either choose a pre-rehearsed routine of poses or respond to challenges with vigorous improvisation. Whatever you do, decide which route you're going to take and *stick to it*.

16 Sailors' tattoos often have particular meanings: a fully rigged ship shows they have sailed round Cape Horn, an

The Pirate Captain grunted.

'Yes. What's that one?' asked Shelley, pointing at his chest. 'Is it a sleepy caterpillar?'

'No,' said the Captain. 'It's a terrifying sea monster.'

'How about this one? Is that a muscly horse?'

'It's a mermaid. Mermaids are unexpectedly hard to draw.'

'And what on earth,' said Mary, 'is *that* meant to be?' She pointed to a series of symbols stretching across the Captain's belly:

'Ah,' said the Captain, following her gaze. 'Actually that one IS a genuine mystery.' He sighed a rueful nostalgic sigh. 'You see, back when I was a lad in Pirating Academy, I had a mad old

anchor indicates they have sailed the Atlantic, a shellback turtle shows they have crossed the Equator, and a full back panel of Kate and Prince William shows they have questionable judgement.

mentor, Calico Jack. Famed as the best pirate from Sussex to Shanghai, but almost preternaturally forgetful. Never remembered to carry any stationery supplies, so whenever anything important came up he tended to use his students as notepads.' The Captain pointed to a line of text etched into the skin just above the symbols –

Here lies the key to every heart's desire!

'See? He was always writing things like that down on us. My left buttock has a note on it reminding him to pick up a prescription.'

'The key to every heart's desire! Why, but that sounds intriguing!' boomed Byron. The pirate with a scarf was starting to wonder if he had any other way of saying words that wasn't 'booming'.

'Yes, but as you can see, unfortunately it's just those gibberish symbols after that,' said the Captain with a shrug.

Mary stroked her chin thoughtfully. 'You've never thought to discover what these symbols might mean?'

'To be honest,' said the Captain, 'I suspect it means he was quite drunk when he tattooed it on me in the first place.'[17]

'You must have some inkling?'

'Not really. I seem to remember a vague story about Calico's grandfather.' The Captain wrinkled his nose as he thought back. 'Gave a lift to this inscrutable European gent, who, one ghostly night during their voyage, after rather too much grog, supposedly told old Calico Senior some profound sort of secret. But that was Calico for you, always arching an eyebrow and saying something enigmatic for no good reason. Probably imagined the whole thing.'

'Well, don't you see?' laughed Byron heartily. 'That's it! That's our adventure! It's been under our noses all this time! Well, under your belly

17   In April 2011, a man in California was convicted of murdering a rival gang member at a liquor store when police noticed that he had a picture of the crime scene tattooed on his chest. The tattoo included the name of the liquor store and a picture of the victim being sprayed by gunfire from a helicopter (a visual metaphor, the man's nickname being 'Chopper').

button, at any rate. A grand quest to uncover the mysterious meaning behind your tattoo!'

'Really? But where would we start? It's just some funny marks,' said the Captain, frowning. 'Isn't it?'

'I don't think it's just some funny marks, Captain,' said Mary, squinting closely at the tattoo. 'I think it must be a *code* of some sort.'

'Exactly!' cried Byron. 'A code! A code that will reveal the key to every heart's desire! All the best adventures have codes in them.'

The Captain contemplated his belly anew. 'A code, eh? Well, fancy that! All this time I thought it was nonsense, and it turns out to be a code. Mystery solved! Who's for cocktails?'

'No, Captain,' said Mary. 'Saying something "is a code" isn't really the hard part. It's the "working out what the code means" bit that's tricky.'

'Oh. Bother.'

Everybody scratched their heads and stared at the Pirate Captain's belly for a while, apart from Shelley, who grimaced, and the pirate in red, who struggled to climb back aboard the boat whilst still stuck in a seal carcass.

'I'm not normally one for body image issues,'

said the Captain, after a couple of wordless minutes had ticked by, 'but I'm starting to feel a little self-conscious now. Could we stare at something else for a bit?'

'It's no use,' said Mary, straightening up with a sigh. 'Runes? Hieroglyphs? I can't make head or tail of it.'

'No,' agreed Byron. 'It's a tricky one. Not really suited to our artistic skillset.'

'Ah well,' said the Captain. 'How about an adventure sitting around in deckchairs instead?'

Byron shook his head. 'We're not defeated yet, Captain. Because I think I know just the fellow who could help us!'

'Oh good grief,' said Shelley, his face clouding over. 'You don't mean . . .'

'I do!' Byron leapt onto a barrel, and stared meaningfully at the horizon, like he was on a book jacket or something. 'Pirate Captain, we must set sail for London!'

'London?' the Captain puffed out his cheeks. 'You realise that sailing from Switzerland to London is more geographically challenging than it sounds? Might add to the expenses.'

'Expenses be damned!' roared Byron.

The Captain beamed again. 'Of all the cele-brated historical characters we have ever met, you are easily my favourites.'

Six

TWO TICKETS TO THE CORPSE FACTORY

The pirates were glad to find that London hadn't changed much since their last visit. They didn't like change – partly because it reminded them of their own inescapable mortality, and partly because it meant having to buy new guidebooks, which were really expensive. The city was still stuffed full of flickering gas lamps and soot-covered fog machines and smiling commuters and little match girls setting fire to Beefeaters.

As Byron led them through the streets of Marylebone, the crew murmured excitedly to each other, because in all their years of creeping towards the lairs of mysterious figures, this was the first time they had ever crept towards the lair of a mathematician. But when they got there, instead of arriving at a mind-bending mathematical plane of reality, they found themselves faced with a perfectly plain terraced house, and, rather than an optical illusion of impossible stairs, there was a regular set of five whitewashed steps leading to the door. There weren't even any henchmen dressed as numbers, just a grumpy butler who rolled his eyes when he saw Byron.

'Are you sure he's a mathematician?' said the Pirate Captain, sensing his lads' disappointment. 'It's not the kind of place I'd expect to find a man from such a glamorous and thrilling profession.'

'No, it's very strange,' explained Byron, as the grumpy butler ushered them into the hallway. 'He's something of a maverick. Some while ago he turned his back on the heady, live-fast-die-young world of the maths establishment, and adopted an entirely different approach to the subject. It's best if you let me do the talking, because he's so staid and unadventurous that if he realises you're a pirate I suspect his head might explode from the shock of it all.'

'You don't honestly think he could see through my disguise?' asked the Pirate Captain, incredulous. In those days piracy was frowned on as a profession, and the beady-eyed London police force lurked on every street corner, so, as always when visiting the Big Smoke, the pirates were in disguise. The crew were all disguised as stern Victorian nannies, while the Pirate Captain was disguised as a sexy fireman. He was adamant that this was because there hadn't been enough Victorian nanny costumes to go around.

'He doesn't get many callers,' said Byron with a shrug, 'and I'm fairly sure he never gets visits from sexy firemen. He may be boring, but he's terribly smart.'

'What is it *this* time, Byron?' An irritable voice floated out from one of the rooms. 'Do you require help counting your toes again? Dividing up a cake? Telling the time?'

When he stepped out into the hallway the owner of the voice appeared just as irritable as he sounded. He polished his glasses, and blinked at his visitors myopically, looking like a cross owl or, in nautical terms, a poorly tuna fish. He scowled so hard that for a moment the Pirate Captain was worried he would scowl his face into a little brown walnut. He'd seen it happen before. Or at least he thought he had. He didn't remember everything perfectly.

Byron gave the man a cheerful punch on the

shoulder. 'Hello, Babs! Admit it. My visits are the only colour in your drab little life. Everybody, I'd like you to meet Charles Babbage. Babbage, I'd like you to meet my new friends. You already know Shelley here. And this is his fiancée, Miss Mary Godwin. These are some stern Victorian nannies, and this is my close friend, a sexy fireman. You may recognise him from the best-selling calendar last Christmas.'

The Pirate Captain was relieved to see that Babbage's calendar featured sexy logarithm tables rather than firemen. The mathematician sighed and waved them into his study.[18] It was choc-a-bloc with clutter, but the room's most striking feature was a huge complicated machine, covered in dials, numbers and brass cogs. Hundreds and hundreds of cogs, all whirring and clicking back and forth like nobody's business.

---

18 To save some time, instead of wasting ages reading a lengthy description of Babbage's study, you can just read the description of the Pirate Captain's cabin from *An Adventure With Scientists* and replace 'pictures of the Pirate Captain' with 'pictures of equations', 'biscuits' with 'half-eaten sandwiches' and 'nautical accoutrements' with 'piles of slide-rules'.

'That's a lot of cogs,' said the Pirate Captain politely.

'Damn straight it's a lot of cogs,' said Babbage.

'Is it some sort of trouser press?' Mary gave the contraption a bit of a poke.

'No, it is not some sort of trouser press. It is a *difference engine*. A mechanical brain, if you will. Not something a poet or a sexy fireman could really be expected to understand. Please don't touch it.'

Babbage pointed sternly to where he'd taped a cardboard sign onto the wall:

Babbage's Three Laws of Difference Engines

*First Law: A difference engine
must have at least six cogs.*

*Second Law: A difference engine
must be able to operate a loom.*

*Third Law: A difference engine must be able
to kill a man, should the mood so take it.*

Hands Off!

'It's very impressive, Mister Babbage,' said Jennifer, smiling sweetly. Jennifer was good with people.

'TEACH ME WHAT IT IS TO BE HUMAN,' said the pirate with gout, doing a difference engine voice. A few of the other pirates giggled, until a glower from Babbage made them stop and stare at the floor.[19] The mathematician went back to studying his blackboard. 'Now, tell me your problem and then shoo.'

'Well, you know how it is,' said Byron, looking around hopefully for some gin. 'A man with my hair and physique mustn't trouble himself with numbers. They're literally poison to me. Did I ever tell you how I once caught consumption simply from being in the same room as a times table?'

'Oooff,' Babbage sighed again. 'Do get *on* with it, man.'

'Now, Babs, if you're going to be like that,' said Byron, 'then perhaps we'll take my friend's

---

19 In the 1860s Babbage became known as a notorious curmudgeon for his vigorous campaign against noisy children rolling hoops in the street.

mysterious code elsewhere . . .' He winked at the Pirate Captain.

Babbage straightened up a bit, equations apparently forgotten.

'Did you just say "mysterious code"?' For the first time since they arrived, he almost made eye contact. 'Well why didn't you say so in the first place?' He hurried over to shut the door, then turned to face the Pirate Captain. 'I do apologise, sexy fireman. I get quite wrapped up in my numbers, and Byron's maths questions are usually so frivolous that I want to tear my hair out and eat it. But I do love puzzles! And codes are the best kind.[20] Can my butler get you anything? A cup of tea? What do sexy firemen normally drink? Let me take that hose, it looks rather heavy. Sit! Sit!'

'Oh, no offence taken,' said the Captain. 'We all have our little obsessions. As a sexy fireman, I'm really into sexy fires.'

---

20   If you like codes you should consider a visit to Bletchley Park, which has lots of interesting exhibits about code-breaking and spies, as well as a ZX Spectrum +2 that plays 'Popcorn' on a constant loop.

'Yes, and numbers are so marvellous!' said Babbage, not really listening. His cross owl face had become rather animated, and now looked like an owl who had just awoken from a nice dream about mouse heads. 'You can do anything with numbers. Did you know that at the heart of everything there lies a mathematical formula that explains it?'

Byron flounced into a huge armchair and put his feet up on an abacus. 'Not this again!'

'Honestly, Mister Babbage,' said Shelley, shaking his head. 'Do you really think you can explain the maelstroms of the human heart with your confounded algebra?! Ridiculous.'

Babbage ignored them. Byron took the hint and decided to occupy himself by pulling stuffing from the chair and using it to make funny eyebrows.

'Yes. So, this code. Could I see it?'

The Pirate Captain started to unbutton his shirt. Babbage's face instantly creased back into a scowl. 'For pity's sake! Not *another* strippogram! Will you never tire of this prank, Byron?! Get out, the lot of you!'

'No, wait, you've got it wrong,' explained the Pirate Captain. 'I haven't done a strippogram for well over a year now. It's simply that the code is a tattoo on my belly, put there by my old pirate mentor when I was at college.'

'What was a pirate mentor doing at Fireman's College?' said Babbage.

The Pirate Captain tried to think fast. Should he say it was a cultural exchange? Pretend he hadn't heard? Feign rabies? Before he could come up with a clever answer, he realised his mouth was already talking.

'I'm not really a sexy fireman,' said the Pirate Captain, 'I'm a Pirate Captain.'

The crew all covered their ears and waited for Babbage's head to explode. To the mathematician's credit, his head remained intact and his face pretty much unmoved.

'That explains the skull and crossbones on your fireman's helmet. And I was wondering when the fire brigade had replaced their traditional axe with a cutlass. Also, you do smell rather of cannons and crow's nests. But please – go on.'

The Pirate Captain tore off his shirt and

pointed a dramatic and nicely manicured finger at the tattoo. Babbage leaned forward and peered through his eyeglasses. For a moment there was no noise except the occasional clunking of cogs emanating from his machine. 'I think,' he said eventually, 'that I have an idea.'

Byron slapped his thigh. 'See, Pirate Captain! I told you he was good. Dull as ditchwater and plain as a potato, but damned clever.'

'You said you got this tattoo when you were at college? I presume that was some time ago?'

'Ages,' the Captain clicked his tongue thoughtfully. 'Back when I used to wear those trousers with penguins all over them. Height of fashion at the time. I think they were supposed to glow in the dark when you were hot, but I never saw it work. Perhaps I washed them on the wrong temperature and all the glow-in-the-dark juice came out. Hard to say.'

Babbage gave the Pirate Captain the faint smile that very clever people do when they're trying desperately not to patronise you. 'Would I be right in thinking that you've indulged yourself with a few feasts since college? Mixed grills? Hams fried in butter? That sort of thing?'

'Once in a while.'

Babbage leaned forward and grabbed the Captain's belly with both hands.

'Steady on!'

'If you'll observe,' said Babbage, stretching out the Captain's belly skin with a sharp yank, 'half the mysterious symbols were simply obscured by this roll of fat. It's actually some numbers!'

Sure enough, when everybody peered at his midriff the code was transformed:

$$204.172$$

'Good grief!' exclaimed Shelley. 'He's right!'

'Not quite correct, Babbage,' said the Pirate Captain. 'Technically I think that's a *washboard ab* rather than a *roll of fat*, but you're spot on about the numbers. Mystery solved! Who's for cocktails?'

'Actually, Captain, that's only a quarter of the mystery solved,' said Mary. 'It's still just some numbers.'

'Bother,' said the Pirate Captain.

'So what can the numbers mean?' puzzled Byron. 'Combination to a safety deposit box? Co-ordinates for a hidden Bacchanalian isle where the lakes are made of whisky and the girls don't know about inhibitions? The measurements of some improbable beauty?'

'No, Byron, none of those,' said Babbage, crossing to a bookcase and pulling out a volume at random. 'Rather more prosaic than that. You see?' He pointed to the book, which had a similar row of numbers to the ones scrawled across the Captain's belly printed on the spine. 'It is a library catalogue number. More precisely, these numbers are the code used by the greatest library in the world – the Bodleian, in Oxford!'

A few of the pirate crew did 'ooh' and 'ahh' noises, because it seemed appropriate, and they didn't know what a library was.

'Well that makes no sense at all,' said the Captain, buttoning his shirt back up. 'I don't see how the key to every heart's desire can be a *book*. Neptune's pants, I hope this isn't going to be like the time Calico Jack's ultimate treasure turned out to be some nonsense about a child's smile. I'm sorry, I should have warned you that he was prone to that sort of thing. Though it's too late for a refund, if that's what you're thinking.'

'A book!' Byron clapped his hands, delighted. 'A search for a mysterious book! This adventure gets better and better!'

The Captain suddenly remembered that the Romantics thought books were the bee's knees, and so he tried to look a bit happier about the revelation. 'Yes, don't get me wrong,' he said, waggling his fireman's hose at Mary. 'Books are great. And not just for propping up wonky table legs. I was assuming the key to every heart's desire would probably be a sapphire the size of a baby, but thinking about it this is *even better*. And possibly it's one of those books with a fancy binding that has gigantic sapphires stuck to the cover, which of course would be the best of both worlds.'

'So!' cried Byron happily. 'The next chapter of our journey! Come on, Babs, pack your suitcase – we must hasten to Oxford!'

'We?' Babbage raised his eyebrows. 'Why on earth do *I* have to come along?'

'Who knows what further mysterious codes there might be to decipher along the way? Think of yourself as a portable calculator,' said Byron with a shrug. 'Also, having a visually uninspiring type like you along on our adventure should really help throw my swashbuckling countenance into sharp relief. You know, like a pig next to a swan.'

'Oh, fair enough,' said Babbage.

Seven

A MONSTROUS CLACKING

And so the pirate boat sailed up the Thames towards Oxford. Because they were bang in the middle of an electrifying quest for a mysterious book, they didn't stop to admire the cultural highlights of either Slough or Didcot. But to pass the time between feasts – which now featured the sort of food the pirates supposed a mathematician might like, such as pies that tessellated and toast cut up into the shape of graphs – Byron gave the crew tips on how best to walk with a continental swagger, Percy and Babbage engaged in heated arguments about whether a really long word was better than a really big number, and Mary sat quietly in a deckchair, apparently scribbling away in a journal. Everybody seemed to be enjoying themselves, except for the Pirate Captain, who had shut himself away in his cabin and hadn't been seen for most of the day.

Jennifer – who, being a former Victorian lady was a bit sharper than the others at picking up on emotional goings-on aboard the boat – gingerly knocked at the Captain's door and poked her head inside, worried that something might be amiss. She was surprised to find him stretched out in his hammock, poring over a big leather-bound book of poetry.

'Are you feeling okay, Captain?' asked Jennifer. She had never seen the Pirate Captain reading a book without prominent anthropomorphic animals on the cover before. 'Byron's about to run through his best brooding faces, if you'd like to come and watch?'

The Captain peered up at her. 'Oh, that's nice. But I think I'll give it a miss. I'm feeling a touch off colour.' He gave his belly a rueful pat. 'Seems that last feast disagreed with me.'

Jennifer gasped. 'You never disagree with feasts, Pirate Captain! You always get on with feasts incredibly well.'

'Well, my stomach is feeling very odd indeed.'

'Odd? What sort of "odd"?'

The Captain flared a nostril miserably. 'You remember our adventure in that meadow? When I was skipping along with my mouth open and accidentally swallowed all those butterflies? It feels a lot like that.'

Jennifer's frown grew deeper, though she still looked pretty. She put a hand on his forehead to see if he was running a temperature. 'What's that you're reading, Captain?'

'It's a book of sonnets. Heavy going, if you must know. Thirty sonnets in and not a single character has pulled out a pistol or got bitten by a poisonous spider. In fact there *aren't* even any characters to speak of. And half the descriptions of things are actually descriptions of *other things* entirely. It's baffling.'

'So why are you reading it?'

The Captain sighed, slammed the book shut and pouted wistfully out of the porthole. 'I thought it might help me come across as a literary type. Oh! I suppose there's no use trying to hide it any longer. It's Mary! The fact is . . . I think I'm in love.'

Jennifer breathed a sigh of relief, because she'd seen this sort of stuff before, back in her old, much more boring life of dinner parties and lace doilies and emotional misunderstandings. 'Oh, is *that* all? I was scared it might be cholera or something.' Love was certainly better than cholera, though maybe a little worse than whooping cough. 'I wouldn't worry, Captain. You know how you tend to get over these things surprisingly quickly. You fell in love three times last month, and one of those was just Black Bellamy in a wig.'

'To be fair to me, he really suited being a redhead. And yes, it's true that in the past I've proved reassuringly resilient when it comes to matters of the heart,' agreed the Captain. 'But this feels . . . different.'

'Different?'

'Well, you know how it usually goes. Meet a girl. Rattle my buckles. Up a staircase backwards, spot of the dashing cutlass business, bosoms heave, I swear eternal commitment and then a week later I get bored and maroon them on a desert island.[21] But, I don't really feel like doing any of that with Mary.'

'What *do* you feel like doing?'

---

21 Bartholomew Roberts used to euphemistically refer to marooning as 'being made a governor of an island'.

'Sighing, mostly. Taking long sorrowful walks. Writing her name on my desk. That sort of thing.'

The Captain pointed to his desk, where he'd scratched the words 'Mrs Mary Captain' a couple of dozen times into the weathered oak.

'I think the problem,' said Jennifer, knowledgeably, 'is that you've got the *unrequited* type of love, which is easily the most annoying kind. But it's probably just all this talk about romance that's to blame. You've got swept away by the atmosphere.'

'Do you think so?' The Captain perked up a bit. 'Yes, maybe that's it. I hope you're right, for all our sakes. You know what happens when I get tangled up in a maelstrom of emotions. It plays havoc with the beard.'

'Anyway, Captain, I don't think you should try to change who you are,' said Jennifer, indicating the book of sonnets. 'You should be true to yourself. Us girls like it when boys are genuine.'

'Ah, now, that might be true enough. But I think you'll find that the *genuine* me is the me who would pretend to be really into all this sort of nonsense in order to convince a girl that we had something in common. QED.'

Jennifer looked stumped, because this certainly did sound like the kind of thing the genuine Pirate Captain would do. Before she had a chance to come up with a counter argument, Byron crashed through the door like a big flouncy labrador.

'My hair is looking astounding today!' he bellowed. 'Also, we've arrived!'

They parked the pirate boat next to some punts, and everybody gathered on deck. Tourists and students ambled about in a work-shy sort of way as the afternoon sun glinted off Oxford's ivory towers. More recently established universities built their towers of brick, but Oxford used ivory, because back in those days people didn't realise that slaughtering thousands upon thousands of whales and elephants to build student accommodation wasn't very ethical.

'Oxford!' said Shelley, looking with disdain at

the pointy skyline. 'My bête noire! My old stony-faced enemy!'

'Do you not like Oxford, Mister Shelley?' asked the pirate in green. 'I think it seems very pretty.'

'I was a student here,' the poet explained, with a sniff. 'Until they expelled me, unable to cope with my radical ideas.'

'What sort of radical ideas did you have?'

'Oh, all sorts,' said Shelley, sounding vague. 'I published numerous shocking pamphlets that threatened to knock the world off its axis.'

'I've had radical ideas too,' nodded the Captain. 'I once made up an entirely new word for "pancakes". Can't remember what it was now, but it didn't catch on. Still, you've got to try these things, haven't you?'

'My ideas were rather more radical, Captain,' said Shelley. His voice dropped to a whisper. 'Amongst other things I proposed the use of some quite unexpectedly bohemian fonts in the university newspaper. Though I fear I have already said too much.'

The Captain suddenly did the face that

indicated either a thought or a cannonball had struck him. 'Expelled, eh? Well now,' he said, with a sly arch of his beetling brow, 'I imagine a dangerous individual such as yourself would probably be a wanted man round these parts. Public Enemy Number One? Hounded by the authorities, that kind of thing?'

'Yes,' said Shelley, looking quite pleased. 'I suppose I would.'

'And we can't risk you getting clapped in irons, can we? Or whatever the academic equivalent of getting clapped in irons is. You're much too valuable to this entire enterprise. So I think it best if you stay onboard the boat for this bit of the adventure.'

Percy shrugged. 'Oh, well. I suppose that *does* make sense.'

'Also, I think it's important for our expedition to maintain a low profile, lest any shadowy figures should also be after this book.'

'Shadowy figures?' said Mary, her ears pricking up.

'Oh yes. In my experience there are always shadowy figures involved when you're on a mission searching for a mysterious thing. So, with that in mind, I think Byron shouldn't come with us either.'

'Me?' cried Byron, on the verge of tears. 'But why?'

The Captain did an apologetic mouth-shape. 'It's just that a fellow of your celebrity is pretty much bound to attract unwanted attention.'

'Confound it!' Byron thumped the boat's railing. 'But you're right. Why, just last week I was almost smothered to death under a mountain of discarded undergarments, my only crime being to walk a little too close to the open window of a nunnery. Damn my dangerously potent pheromones.'[22]

'I can't really think of a reason that Babbage shouldn't come,' the Captain continued, 'except I believe I heard that there's an exhibition of calculating devices at the University Museum. From what I've been told, if you turn some of

_____

22   Byron's wife, Annabella, coined the term 'Byromania' to refer to the commotion his presence would cause. Keenly aware of his image, Byron made sure that any portraits showed him doing dramatic things rather than writing.

them upside down you can write the words "BOOBLESS" and "SHOE BILE". '

'Ooh,' said Babbage. 'I wouldn't want to miss that.'

'So, I guess it's down to me and you, Mary,' said the Captain, pulling on his fireman's coat and marching down the gangplank. 'Just the two of us. Same as those sleuthing duos you read about in magazines. I'm like the hard-bitten senior detective, with just his final case to solve, and you're like my feisty new canine partner, with your shining nose and eager manner. Or possibly I'm like a disorganised slob who never made lieutenant and you're like the buttoned-down humourless Russian who doesn't approve of my louche attitude but has been assigned to work with me for diplomatic reasons. One of those.'

Eight

PHANTOMS?
PHANTOMS.
PHANTOMS!

'Of course, the really dangerous thing about university libraries is the simmering sexual tension,' whispered the Pirate Captain, as he and Mary joined the queue for the Bodleian's information desk.

'Are you sure?' asked Mary. She looked around the place. In front of them two prematurely balding students quietly discussed what the best type of hole-punch might be. Over in the corner a postgraduate worried about his career prospects. Somewhere, a don snored.

'Yes, it's the atmosphere of forced restraint combined with young people at their most frisky age. Creates a crackling aura of pent-up hormones.'

'If you say so, Pirate Captain,' said Mary, doing her pretty eye-rolling trick again.

'Anyhow,' continued the Captain. 'This is exciting, isn't it? Here we are, edging closer to solving my enigmatic belly riddle.'

'Of course, we might have edged a bit faster if you hadn't insisted on that bucolic punt ride to get here. Or the champagne picnic in Port Meadow. Or the gentle stroll through the Botanic Gardens. Which was all lovely, of course, but did seem like a long detour.'

'Can't be too careful. I thought it best to blend in with the tourists. Lest those shadowy figures I made up earlier should be spying on us.' The Captain held up a punnet of strawberries left over from the picnic. 'Would you like me to feed you some more strawberries?'

Mary patted her stomach and pulled a face. 'Actually, I'm quite full of strawberries now. But thanks anyway.'

'I happen to know a sonnet about straw-berries. Would you like to hear it?' The Captain cleared his throat.

'Gosh. Another sonnet already? Maybe you should save it for later,' Mary said, smiling through slightly gritted teeth. Then, not want-ing to be rude, she quickly added, 'Don't get me wrong, though. It's certainly impressive how many sonnets you've got more-or-less memorised.' She stifled a yawn. 'It's like a whole other side to you I would never have guessed at.'

The Captain brightened at this, and decided now might be a good time to use the latest metaphor he had been working on. Obviously this wasn't the first time the Captain had attempted a metaphor – there was that one about ravening wolves which hadn't really panned out a few adventures back – but this one was about a jewel, and he knew a lot about jewels, so was more confident that he'd nailed it.

'Another side to me? Yes, I suppose in many ways, you could say I'm like a *jewel* with myriad *facets*, each one more unexpected than the next.'

'Do you think? Well, that's certainly an interesting point of view.'

'But do you know what makes a jewel shine all the more brilliantly? I don't mean the jewel's setting, with all the cherubs and the gold leaf, which is, metaphorically speaking, my crew. And I don't mean "good lighting" either because that's too obvious.'

Mary sighed. 'Enlighten me, Captain. I hope you're not going to say "a second radiant jewel set alongside it, so they might share in one another's glow" because that's the kind of mushy nonsense that Shelley spouts when he's drunk.'

'Ah,' said the Pirate Captain, 'give me a moment.' The queue shuffled forward.

'It's good lighting,' said the Pirate Captain eventually. Mary looked like she was about to say something, but to the Captain's relief they'd reached the front of the queue and the librarian was peering up at them with a quizzical expression.

'Hello there,' said the Pirate Captain. 'I'm doing a thesis about firefighting for my fireman's exams, and I wonder if you could help me out.' He started to unbutton his shirt.

'Stop! Stop! Have you gone mad?' cried the librarian in a whisper. 'Are you trying to ratchet up the sexual tension in here any further? Can't you feel we're almost at bursting point?!' Across the room some dust fell from a professor's head onto a book about Early Modern French Land Reforms. 'Good God, man! Put that tempting belly away!'

'Sorry,' said the Pirate Captain. 'It's just that I've got a tattoo I've recently discovered is actually a catalogue number for a book in this library. So I need to show you at least a sliver of my midriff, but I'll try to keep it as drab and sexless as possible. See?'

The librarian leaned over his desk and scrutinised the Pirate Captain's belly skin.

'Underneath the tired-looking caterpillar tattoo?'

The Pirate Captain was about to ask what was so wrong with everybody that they couldn't tell the difference between 'a caterpillar who was tired' and 'a sea serpent who was furious because tiny sailors were firing a cannon at her eggs'. But he didn't want to do a whining voice in front of Mary, so he just did a pouty nod instead.

'Well, that'll be somewhere on the second floor,' said the librarian. 'Straight up those stairs.'

'Can we just go up there? We don't have to join the library or anything? I brought two forms of ID.'

'You just have to swear a solemn oath that

you're not planning to set any books on fire or draw genitals in the margins.'

'Are *breasts* genitals?' asked the Pirate Captain.

'I don't think so,' said Mary.

'In that case, I'm happy to swear as much as you like.'

'Up you go!' said the librarian cheerfully.[23]

The Bodleian Library had a copy of every book ever published on every subject you could think of: interesting subjects like creatures, dull subjects like cowboys, worthwhile subjects like medicine, pointless subjects like innovation strategy and joke subjects like anthropology.

'Particles, pavements, periscopes, pharmacies – oh look, they've even got a *pirates* section!' exclaimed Mary, as they wandered along the vast canyon of shelves. The Pirate Captain froze mid-stride, and turned a bit ashen, which means that

---

23 The fourth – and fairly ineffectual – Bodleian librarian was Thomas Lockey, a man who died of a 'surfeit of cherries', one of the best ways to go.

the colour drained from his face, not that he dissolved into a powder. 'Good grief! They've got an *entire shelf* of your work!' Mary gasped. 'I think I owe you an apology, Pirate Captain. When you said that you'd written several books, I have to admit that I assumed you were . . . well . . . *embellishing.*'

The Captain *had* done a fair bit of embellishing in his time: claiming to be a former bullfighter; his invention of ice-cream; his love of opera; drinking the Thames dry; having three extra nipples; being able to run faster than a cheetah; never having worn make-up; liking purple better than blue; the coastline of Sardinia being based on his profile; eating sheet metal; owning the world's largest collection of saucy postcards; his refusal to be taken for a fool – none of these things were entirely true. So he didn't think any less of Mary for doubting him, because you should try to see the best in people.

'I hope you can forgive me, Pirate Captain.'

'Yes, forgive and forget, water under the boat, no time to dwell on all that now anyway,' said the Captain, suddenly businesslike. 'Let's not hang about. We don't want to let those shadowy figures steal a march on us. Chop chop!'

'Hang on a second,' Mary frowned and reached up for one of the Captain's books. He did his best to get in the way, but she was a bit too quick.

'I thought,' said Mary, looking at the cover, 'that you said your books were about emotions? Lyrical landscapes? Waves crashing on a rocky shore?'

She held up the copy of *Barnacles Never Sleep (Despite Appearances)*, and pointed at the lurid cover illustration, which showed a fulsome lady in a bikini being ravished by some fascist barnacles. The Captain hefted his biggest sigh of the adventure so far.

'Oh, look, there's not much point pretending any more – Mary, I've got a confession to make.' He stared unhappily at his shiny boots. 'The fact is, my published output isn't particularly literary at all. Apart from the biography that I wrote to spite Napoleon, the philosophical masterwork that I wrote after a bet with Karl Marx, and the steamy potboiler that I wrote to attract a great white whale, all the rest are pretty much lowest common denominator penny-dreadful schlock. I only really took it up as a hobby because I'd been incorrectly informed that authors are the best-paid people in the world. One reviewer described my work as "both borderline incomprehensible and unceasingly vacuous".' He pointed at the quote on the back of *Barnacles Never Sleep*. 'Also, whilst I'm confessing things, I might as well admit that I don't actually understand a single word of those sonnets I've been regaling you with.'

Mary bit her lip. 'It did sort of seem like you were reading them out phonetically.'

They both fell silent. For a while the only sound they could hear was the noise of books resting on shelves, which wasn't really enough of a sound to distract them from the awkwardness of the moment.

'Captain,' said Mary, gravely. 'I've got a secret too.'

'Oh hellfire, you're not Black Bellamy in a wig, are you?'

'No, Pirate Captain, I'm not. But the truth

is . . . I don't really care for all that poetic stuff either.'

'You don't?'

'No. I mean, I *try*. And Percy is a genius, he really is. But I just can't help myself. I long for books where things *happen*. You know . . . thrilling chases. Gothic mansions, and above all . . .' Her eyes lit up like candles – that being one of the only things that eyes could light up like before Edison – and she almost whispered the word, 'Monsters!'

'Monsters?'

'Oh! I know! It's ridiculous! I'm so ashamed.' Mary buried her face in her hands, suddenly dejected. 'I don't know what's wrong with me. The worst thing is, I've even taken to writing one myself. A novel, I mean. Please don't tell the others. Percy would think I'd lost my mind.'

The Captain looked confused, and then his pleasantly weathered face broke into a big grin. 'But – I feel exactly the same way! Almost all my books have monsters in them. Look . . .' He pulled a second book from the shelf. 'This one is about a diabolical space cactus.' He pulled another down. 'This one is about a nameless blob that eats children.' And another. 'And this one has a terrible fungus in it. The good thing about a terrible fungus is that you don't really have to worry about its motivation.'

'These look fantastic!' exclaimed Mary.

'Most of the time I tend to go for either the fungus or a giant sentient clam. What sort of monsters do you like?'

'Well,' said Mary, 'I was thinking a hideous half-man, half-seaweed mutant might be the way to go.'

'Good choice. Can't go wrong with mutants. Saves you the bother of an origin story if you just say "it's a mutant". '

Mary's whole face shone. 'Oh, Captain, you don't know what a relief it is to be able to talk to somebody about all this!'

Soon they'd both forgotten the entire point of being in the library in the first place. As Mary pored over the colour illustrations in *The Sponge*

that Stood Still and *My First Mate was a Zombu-loid*, a strand of loose hair fell across her cheek. The Pirate Captain reached out to brush it back. Suddenly he felt his hand turn to jelly. Normally when he used that expression he was mucking about with the lads, pretending to be a 'were-jelly' when the moon was full. But this time it was because of *an emotion*, which in many ways was more terrifying than any werejelly could ever be.

'Let me get that strand of hair for you,' he said.

There was a creaking noise. The Captain hadn't had as much experience brushing pretty girls' strands of loose hair back into place as he liked to pretend, so at first he thought maybe Mary's face was creaking. But then the towering bookshelf wobbled alarmingly. It pitched backwards, forwards . . . and suddenly an avalanche of books came crashing down right on top of them. The last thing the Pirate Captain saw before he pushed Mary out of harm's way was a copy of Black Bellamy's autobiography – *Swash-buckled!* – smacking him right in the eye.

Nine

THE CANNIBAL
HAMMOCK

'Kraken's ears!' roared the Pirate Captain, flouting library etiquette. He rubbed the rapidly swelling bump on his head and looked about for his hat as Mary finished digging him out from the pile of books.

'Isn't this thrilling!' said Mary, with a grin. 'Almost killed by your own prose! Byron will go mad with jealousy. And look!'

She led the Captain behind the toppled bookcase and pointed to an incriminating ladder.

'I don't think it was an accident! I think it was foul play! Somebody *pushed* that bookcase! It seems you were right about those shadowy figures all along!'

'Good grief,' said the Captain. 'I mean to say, obviously I'm no stranger to attempts on my life: jealous husbands, cowboy assassins, exotic femmes fatales. But even so – you don't expect this sort of thing in a place of learning. It's what my old Aunt Joan would have described as "a bit much". She would have probably gone on to blame gypsies, because she was slightly racist. Different generation.'

'Well, obviously *somebody* doesn't want us to get our hands on this mysterious book!'

'The mysterious book!' The Captain slapped his forehead. Without the pirate with a scarf around to write him useful little reminders he did kind of have a tendency to lose track of his adventures.

They dusted themselves down and hurried on through the maze of shelving.

'Paedocracy, phengophobia, philately . . .' Mary ticked off the subjects as they went. 'Ah, here we are: two oh four . . . ooh! It's the *philosophy* section.'

She darted forward, running her finger along the shelves.

'Two oh four one oh four . . . Here it is!' She pulled out a large book, and coughed as a cloud of dust billowed up from the cracked old binding.

'Oh,' said Mary, peering at it. 'That's not really what I was expecting at all.'

There, picked out in fancy gold lettering, was the title:

'A-ha. Plato,' said the Captain knowledgeably. 'He's the one who thinks reality is somebody making dinosaur shadows on the wall of a cave, isn't he? Or is he the one who's always jumping out of baths because he's trodden on a cork-screw? I get muddled.'

'He's the dinosaur-shadows-in-a-cave one,' said Mary.[24]

The Captain gave the book a shake, hoping that a treasure map would fall out, or maybe a really nice bookmark. He didn't think a book-mark would really count as 'the key to every heart's desire' but sometimes in life you have to take what you can get.

'Hang on a second,' said Mary, grabbing the book back, and flicking to near the middle. 'Look here! There's a whole chunk missing!'

'Probably weevils. We get them on the boat

---

24 Aristotle said more stupid things than Plato. Gems include the theory that rats spring fully formed from mud, and that eels are a type of dewdrop.

and they're hungry little devils. If you leave a plate of ship's biscuits out and so much as turn your back, they're gone in ten minutes flat. Apart from ship's pink wafers. The weevils aren't so keen on those.'

'I don't think this is the work of weevils. Someone has got here before us! Do you think it can have been the shadowy figure?'

'Not very likely,' said the Pirate Captain, eyeing the book carefully. 'You see, one perk of my frankly poor domestic regime is that I'm a bit of an expert at dust accumulation rates. And I should say this book hasn't been touched for at least a hundred years.'

Mary scratched her ear thoughtfully. The Captain realised that even her ears were attractive. Usually ears freaked him out a bit, because of the way they went all the way to your brain, but he could imagine spending a lot of happy evenings staring at Mary's ears without any difficulty at all.

'Oh dear,' she sighed, at a loss. 'So what do we do now?'

'I'm afraid the trail has gone cold,' said the Pirate Captain. 'In my books, this is a point where the hero thinks that the adventure is over and they'd better give up and go back to architecting or catching rats, depending on which day job I've chosen for him. It's what I call a *moment of crisis*.'

'We don't really have day jobs in the Romantics,' said Mary. 'And your job *is* having adventures.'

'Not to worry,' said the Pirate Captain. 'When the trail goes cold I always have a character walk into the room and shout the next clue. So, given that art imitates life, I suspect we just need to wait.'

Mary and the Captain waited. Mary started to hum a little tune, and the Captain did his best to will another strand of her hair to come loose, so he could try his brushing-it-back-into-place trick again, but nothing seemed forthcoming. They waited some more.

'On the other hand,' said the Captain eventually. 'Sometimes my books do just sort of stop in the middle.'

'. . . So then we returned here and I ate this bacon,' said the Pirate Captain, finishing off his story and his bacon. They were back aboard the pirate boat, and everybody was sat round the kitchen table listening to the Captain's account of his and Mary's trip to the library. Obviously he'd left out the stuff about Mary's secret love of monsters, and the business with his hand turning to jelly.

'What was a dinosaur doing loose in the Bodleian?' asked Babbage.

Though he had also added a few extra bits to make it more exciting.

'Never mind about the dinosaur,' said Mary. 'Take a look at this!'

She plonked the book down on the table and flicked to the contents page. Shelley and Byron stared at where she was pointing for a moment and then gasped in unison.

'Keats's teeth!' said Byron.

'But – it can't be! Can it? I thought it was a myth!' said Shelley.

'Apparently not!' said Mary.

'You'll have to enlighten the crew I'm afraid,'

said the Pirate Captain, not seeing anything very obviously remarkable about the contents page. 'Some of the lads aren't quite as worldly as the rest of us. Hard to get them to concentrate on philosophical subjects, because it doesn't really suit the piratical personality type.'

Mary jabbed at the title of the missing bit of book. '"On Feelings"!' she said. The pirates went on looking blank-faced.

'It has always been said that Plato once wrote a great, lost Socratic dialogue. The legendary "On Feelings",' said Shelley, taking up the story. 'Plato's subject was the nature of love itself. Supposedly his uncanny treatise unlocked the very mysteries of the human heart to any who read it.'

'Some even say,' said Byron, hunching forward over the table, 'that Plato had discovered a way of impressing a lady so much, that once you knew his secret there wouldn't be a single girl who could resist you, no matter how set in opposition to the idea her heart might at first be.'

The Captain's eyes widened. Though

'heightened' might be a better term, because actually their width remained pretty static. 'You mean to say . . .'

'Yes!' roared Byron. 'It was said to turn any dating situation into the legendary Sure Thing.'

'Neptune's biscuits,' said the Pirate Captain, trying to take it all in. He slumped back in his chair, a bit overwhelmed. The pirate with a scarf fanned him with his hat. 'Could it be possible?'

'Nobody has ever been able to find out! The only copy of "On Feelings" was supposedly destroyed back when the Library of Alexandria burned down in 391 AD. But there have been all sorts of stories about it since then. Translations popping up here and there over the millennia, only to vanish again. Accounts of scandalised monks trying to conceal the potent secret contained within. All that kind of stuff.'

Shelley paced feverishly up and down the length of the cabin.

'Oh! This is so frustrating! I feel like a caged animal!'

'Yes,' agreed the Captain. 'Though not a wolf

or a bear or anything like that. I'd say you were more of a wan dormouse.'

Shelley punched his own palm. 'To think that we're on the brink of such a discovery, yet here I am, trapped on this confounded boat because I'm too much of a threat to the Establishment.'

'Also, don't forget that someone tried to kill your girlfriend. You don't seem particularly concerned about that,' said Jennifer. She mouthed a word that Victorian women aren't supposed to know.

'Of course. Thanks for saving her life and everything, Pirate Captain. Very noble of you.' Shelley put an arm around Mary. 'Anyhow! My mind is made up! It's time Percy Shelley turned his full searing intellect to the matter. I shall plunge my head directly into the lion's maw!'

'The ship's lion wandered off last February,' said the pirate with gout, apologetic.

'According to this,' Shelley continued, indicating where a list of names was pasted into the front cover of the book, 'the last person to borrow the book, some hundred and fifty years ago – was an undergraduate at my old College.

Perhaps that might give us a lead. I shall steal in there, and find out what I can.'

Mary started to put on her coat, but Percy held up an imperious hand.

'No, Mary. I welcome your eagerness, but there are some things a man must do alone.'

'Are you sure?' said the Pirate Captain. 'A few lines about a woman's "pale and anxious brow" aren't much use against a bookshelf-wielding maniac.'

'True, Pirate Captain, but I'm simply too idealistic to let danger get in the way of our prize. Now, I will be requiring some sort of disguise. Ideally something in green, to go with my skin tone.'

The Pirate Captain stroked his beard and crossed over to the dressing-up box.

'Well, let's see what we've got. Tourist? No, bit obvious.'

'Wealthy benefactor?' suggested the pirate with a scarf.

'Visiting matador?' said the pirate in red.

'Polar explorer?' said the pirate who didn't really listen to conversations but couldn't resist contributing anyway.

'Here we go,' said the Pirate Captain. He pulled out a set of dirty overalls and a long hooked pole. 'Drain Technician! Wear these, stick your arms down a few drains and nobody will look twice at you.'

Ten

THE HAUNTED TEETH

While Shelley was gone, everybody else decided to check out the shops and museums of Oxford. They all agreed that although the Ashmolean had a nice display of Etruscan forks, the Pitt Rivers was the best museum by far, mainly because of the shrunken heads. After their trip they stopped off at a little café in Jericho. There was quite an academic air to the party now, because most of the pirate crew had bought themselves university scarves and mortar boards, and the pirate with a hook for a hand even sported a gown that identified him as a Dean of Divinity. Everybody drank their coffee and had an intellectual discourse about what the best way to shrink a head would actually be. Byron thought the best way to shrink a head would be to use some sort of Egyptian curse. The pirate with gout thought you could probably do it by soaking the head in vinegar and then leaving it out in the sun for a while, like a conker.

And Babbage thought you should either use a macaque's head in the first place, or simply remove the skull and then bury the skin in hot sand, because he was the only one who had bothered to read the museum's information card. Before anybody could test their various theories out on one of the cabin boys, the tinkling of the café's bell and a sudden strong smell of drains alerted them to Shelley's return.

'Hello, Percy,' said Byron. 'Any joy?'

Shelley sat down, unbuttoned his overalls, did a little flourish with his hand, and pulled a winsome face. 'Some say there spirits of the air swoop unseen / Amongst humanity's fever'd press to learn.'

'Ye gods. Spare us the verse,' said Babbage, looking at his pocket watch.

Shelley's face went from winsome to cross.

'Sorry. I forgot we've got a philistine in the room who, instead of a heart has a chimney belching logic to an uncaring sky! Fine. It was only an introductory passage anyway. But all right: I will confine myself to the bare facts.'

There are times when it behoves a man to look back on his youth, to revisit the wending path that led to his current station. This was such a time! Please note, I shall occasionally employ the myth of Orpheus to illustrate my passage into the academic underworld. I realise that you pirates may not be familiar with the classics, so I've brought along some copies of Ovid's *Metamorphoses*. Share if there aren't enough to go around. No, there aren't any pictures. Yes, it's in Latin. What? You can't read Ovid in translation! Well, just *listen* then.

As I stood on the threshold of my *alma mater*, I gazed through the portal of ancient Oxford stone and saw reflected back the very depths of my soul. Some of you may have dismissed me as the theoretical, intellectual type who shies away from direct action. You would be mistaken. I am more than capable of launching myself into vigorous gestures. Oft are the occasions when passions must triumph to galvanise the spirit. Yes indeed! 'Shelley's a man who knows what needs doing and when,' they'll say, 'I swear he's a human spark. How we got him wrong!'

As I contemplated my inherent dynamism for a short while, several urchins loitering near the college threshold made chicken movements with their arms, for reasons I could not fathom, perhaps some childish craze. I readied a withering retort, but fortunately for the urchins, a passing pie seller jostled me with his cart and I fell sprawling into the college. A lucky escape for them. I was in!

When Orpheus entered the Underworld, he faced Cerberus the triple-headed hound. No less fearsome was the countenance that manifested itself now. While I was confronted with two fewer heads and it was built with more emphasis on 'whey-faced undergraduate' than 'fearsome canine', here too was a barrier every bit the equal of a mythical dog. Despite a welcoming smile this hellish guardian wore the invisible cloak of hegemony and a shiny badge with the college name written upon it. He told me it was two pennies to get in and for an extra penny I could have a brief history of the college in leaflet form. There were other offers. I am not a man who is easily shaken, but this approach disarmed me. I quite forgot my adopted profession of drainage technician and soon found myself ambling into the sunlit quadrangle clutching a ticket, a leaflet, and a voucher for a penny off at Benny's Chop House on the High Street. Though this had not been my plan, I congratulated myself, and wondered how my Cerberus might feel to know that he had just allowed a dangerous radical into college.

Pardon? The voucher? Yes, you can have it. No, there isn't a menu. I don't know, presumably *chops*? No, I don't know what kind of chops. *Cow chops?* There's no such thing. Can we hold questions until the end? Thank you.

Where was I? Ah yes! The quadrangle. It was just as I remembered. Shafts of bright sunlight, Mother Nature's lifeblood, illuminated motes of scholarly dust. When the younger Shelley took these same tentative steps, he expected to acquaint himself with like-minded souls. 'Let us gather in these places to talk of philosophy,' he had thought. 'Let us speak of a new humanity.' But what did he find? Timid curates-in-waiting, desiccated scholars, mindless milksops and brainless rowers who would rather mock a man's perfectly elegant new trousers than over-turn a bankrupt culture. But I had infiltrated my way in! Who's the 'pale idiot' now? 'Shows little promise' eh, Professor Gilliard?

My reverie was interrupted. 'Hoy! We don't want the likes of you in here!' barked an uncouth Oxford accent. 'Clear out!'

A porter! He prodded me with a stick.

Here was my second obstacle – my River Styx. Page forty-two. This required cunning and guile. I transformed my countenance, adopted a menial expression that does not come naturally to me and eyed a nearby drain.

'Good morrow. I am but a humble drain cleaner with the filth of civilisation foremost in my mind. Behold my rude attire! Savour, if you will, my drainy aroma. Think of me as an uneducated

Heracles, tasked with clearing the Augean stables.' Then I turned the full force of my cunning to bear. 'My assignment? To cleanse the drains 'neath the college records, preferably those that date back to the seventeenth century. Guvnor.'

The rubicund visage scrutinised me for a moment, then split asunder into a broad grin.

'Master Shelley! Why, we haven't seen you in years! I was saying only this morning to Bert, I was saying "we haven't seen Master Shelley in some time, have we?" I did used to enjoy his company. Always a good boy, I said. Never any trouble.' He looked at my outfit. 'Is it Rag Week already? Very good costume.'

Disaster! My innate air of cultivation, so impossible as it is to conceal, combined with the Captain's frankly shoddy disguise – that would be hard pressed to bamboozle a sea-cucumber – risked all. My thoughts were like quicksilver. 'Master Shelley? Be he the poet on everyone's lips? I hear his views are too shocking by half.'

The impudent porter reached out and tweaked my cheek. 'Bless you! That's what you were always saying! Look at your little face, you haven't aged a day! Why, I'll bet you still don't need to shave.'

I only tell you this to emphasise his idiocy. Whether a man needs to shave or not is neither here nor there. Some men are just naturally less hirsute. The ancient Assyrians recognised it as a sign of advanced thinking, I'm informed. I make no comment.

'Be told, man! I am but a simple drain cleaner.'

I received a stagey wink in return. 'Right you are, Master Shelley. Now, you said something about the college records? You'll be wanting the College Secretary's office, through there and up the second staircase. Oh it is nice to see you.'

Rising like a tiger, I stole across to the staircase and crept upwards with a rough-and-ready working-class tread. Upon entering the College Secretary's office, I bowed and waved my drain-cleaning stick.

'Drain technician!'

'Master Shelley!' said the College Secretary. 'I thought you left us after that misunderstanding with the pamphlet? No matter. Have you returned? How lovely! Is it Rag Week already?'

Here was my Hades! Like Orpheus confronting the Lord of the Underworld, I dropped all artifice and fixed him with a look that said I was not a fellow who would take any nonsense.

'How can I help you? It's always nice to see one of our alumni returning. You probably realise that at this time the college is suffering from something of a shortage of funds. We've had to stop serving pheasant for breakfast to the undergraduates altogether. Just five groats a month could ensure a law student receives fresh plover's eggs delivered to his rooms every morning.'

I bargained with him and, by means which I shall not disclose, extracted the following eerie tale. I will now attempt to impersonate his voice.

The College Secretary's Account

It was many centuries ago, a dark time of tights and unflattering haircuts. One Count Ruthven came up to the college during a thunderstorm. He was unremarkable, didn't mingle much, spent rather more time in the library than one would expect from a student. Then after a term, something changed. He became a *seducer*! It is said that he impregnated half the city's young women within the week. Naturally the University authorities couldn't stand for that sort of behaviour, and he was sent down forthwith.

Yes, he did sound that 'growly'. No, he wasn't Geordie. Nor Welsh. Fine, so I can't really do accents. It's not a talent I envy in others. Can I carry on? Good.

By and by, the College Secretary showed me a painting of the new intake from 1677 and indicated the Count. Those eyes! That sickly pallor! A sight I shall take to my grave, so ill-made it was. As I hurried back through the quadrangle, clutching my hard-won bounty to my breast, my heart filled with the ichor of intrigue. Lengthening shadows seemed to chase after me. Not literal shadows, but metaphorical shadows. Shadows that suggest a grim and uncertain future awaits us. This is no fool's errand. For such a gargoyle to seduce so many, there must be dazzling wonders in that elusive tome. So, we must hasten, my friends, to ... Castle Ruthven, Ruthven Pass, Carpathian Mountains, South-Eastern Romania.

'Pretty Romantic stuff, Percy,' said Byron, downing his coffee and then banging the mug on the table.

'Thank you, Byron, I like to think so,' agreed Percy with a theatrical sigh.

Jennifer frowned. 'Mister Shelley. Am I understanding this right? Did you essentially walk into your old college and give them a cash donation in exchange for an address?'

Shelley snapped a hand away from his brow.

'Did you not listen, madam? Orpheus! A three-headed dog! Oh, but you've proven my point – one can reduce the most incredible tale to rational facts and make it sound dull and workaday.'

'What's a "rubicund"?' asked the albino pirate.

'Do "visage", "countenance" and "face" all

mean the same thing? Why not just say "face"?'
said the pirate with gout.

'How can a mote hold dust? I thought they
were full of water,' said the pirate in green.

'Lads! Lads!' said the Pirate Captain, holding
up an admonishing hand. 'Leave the man be!
You're forgetting that not everyone can be a
dashing swashbuckler who eats danger for
breakfast. It's tremendously brave for a lubber
to go and ask a man for an address.'

'And what an address!' said Byron. 'The sort
of address that speaks of dark legends! Moonlit
passes! Unnatural goings-on! We haven't a
moment to lose!'

Everybody cheered and, for the last time in
this adventure, they were all smiling, even the
pirate with a prosthetic wooden bottom-half-
of-his-head.

The happy mood was spoiled a few minutes
later when the adventurers arrived back at the
pirate boat. It looked pretty shabby at the best of

times, seeing as it was the front half and back half of two different boats hammered together. But now the boat looked even worse than usual, because there was a big piece of graffiti scrawled right across the side of the battered hull. Whoever had done the graffiti hadn't used paint or a marker pen like you might expect – instead the message appeared to be written in blood:

TURN BACK OR FEEL DEATH'S ICY HAMS!

And underneath that was a rough approximation of a skull saying, 'I DIDN'T TURN BACK AND LOOK WHAT HAPPENED TO ME! THINK ON.'

'Dear me,' said Babbage. 'I don't much like the look of this.'

'Do you think it could be a warning of some sort?' said the pirate who was slow on the uptake.

'What do you suppose "Death's icy hams" could be? It's making me quite hungry,' said the pirate with bedroom eyes.

'I'm not sure that says "hams",' said Mary. 'I

think it's meant to say "HAND". "DEATH'S ICY HAND". You have to cut whoever did this some slack, because it's probably quite tricky to write with dead crows.' She indicated two severed bits of crow discarded on the riverbank.

'It's a rum do,' said the Pirate Captain, trying a new expression, 'but you can't help but admire the ingenuity. Rather like crow crayons. Very inventive.'

Byron slapped his thigh. 'This is the ticket! First an attempted murder in a library, and now a dire warning telling us to back off. A proper adventure! You're a man of your word, Captain!'

'*Should* we turn back?' asked Babbage. 'I have limited experience of awful threats written in crow blood, but it seems like the kind of thing you should probably pay attention to.'

'Turn back?' said the Pirate Captain, already halfway up the gangplank. 'Of course not. You see, the thing is, whoever wrote that warning doesn't know us pirates very well.' He flashed his devil-may-care grin again and winked at Mary. 'Half the crew would sell their own grand-mothers to have a skeleton face.'

Eleven

SCREAM, BARNACLE, SCREAM!

Note found pinned to galley door, pirate boat:

To whom it may concern,

I understand that spirits are running high, and I would be the last to condemn demonstrations of enthusiasm. But since we set sail for the continent the noise on this boat has been untenable. For the past three nights, I have been prevented from sleep by a relentless cacophony of accordions, poetry and bellowing.

So I have taken the liberty of conducting a small experiment. Imagine, if you will, a series of marbles of increasing mass. These are placed on a smooth wooden tray immersed in a shallow pool of water (to correct for the natural rocking motions of the boat). Ignoring negligible air movement in my cabin, we can assume that any motion in the marbles is caused by vibrations induced by sound waves. I have calibrated the escalating movement of marbles (and therefore volume of noise) as 'Silence', 'Acceptable Hush', 'Nuisance' and 'Untenable'. Most nights the noise levels have alternated between 'Acceptable Hush' and 'Nuisance'. I would probably have let this pass. However, last night, a particularly robust bellow (from Lord Byron, I believe) tipped the marbles into 'Untenable'. There is my evidence. You are welcome to inspect the apparatus.

Please be more considerate.

Your cordial travelling companion,

Charles Babbage

Note found pushed under the Captain's door:

Dear Pirate Captain,

Here are the first few chapters of my novel, working title - 'Gorgo: Half-Man, Half-Seaweed!' As a fellow enthusiast for monsters and the macabre I dearly wish to know what you might make of it. Though be gentle with my efforts, for they are but young buds, easily stomped on by shiny pirate boots. And I would beseech you once more to <u>not mention any of this to Percy</u> - it is not his fault, but I fear he would never be able to understand my fixation with such creature-based frivolities.

Love,

Mary

PS: Do you think Garagulon is a better name than Gorgo? I can't decide.

Note found glued to bread bin, pirate boat:

To the bread thief,

Strong words? Perhaps. However - on the last two occasions that I have visited the bread bin, I have seen someone has pilfered a slice from my special loaf of bread.

I am wheat-intolerant. This is the only bread I can eat without inducing numerous unpleasant symptoms. If I run out, then I would be very surprised if the bakers in the local Eastern Mediterranean ports are capable of making a replacement. I anticipate the bread theft will end now? (This is a rhetorical question. I very much wish it to end.)

On an unrelated note, the noise situation has worsened. We had two nights with 'Untenable' interludes (Lord Byron again) and then somebody took my marbles. If the bread thief is also partial to marbles then please return them also.

Your travelling companion,
Charles Babbage

Note found stuck to Mary's hammock:

From the pen of the Pirate Captain

Hiya Mary,

1) Garagulon and Gorgo are both good names. Though I would be inclined to stick with something more mysterious. 'The Beast That Walked Like a Man'? It is always best when something 'walks like a man'. Even when it is just a man.

2) Try using more capital letters. I've always found that a great way to make a scene more dramatic than it would otherwise be is through the liberal use of capital letters and underlining. e.g.: 'A sudden FLASH of lightning made Phoebe GASP. She RUBBED her eyes. Had that been a shape she'd seen, momentarily silhouetted in the WINDOW? The shape of a man? Or rather a shape … NOT QUITE LIKE A MAN?' See?

3) Another good trick is to give every single chapter a surprise twist ending. So, maybe for the end of chapter one you could reveal that your heroine, Phoebe, is actually called Eve, and that your hero, Mr Henderson, is called Adam, and that this is all taking place thousands of years ago on a planet called ... Earth! Other good twists to consider: one where the 'monster' turns out to be beautiful by our standards, it's everybody else who is hideous, except then it turns out no! actually everyone was just <u>wearing masks</u>, so it is the right way around after all. Or one where dinosaurs never existed and that's important somehow.

4) Your paper smells nice, by the way.

5) I have taken the liberty of drawing you a cover illustration. When you eventually send this off to publishers you'll need to have drawn a cover illustration if you want to look like a serious writer. I realise your story doesn't involve a bear but I'm pretty good at bears, so I put one in anyway.

THE KELP THAT WALKED LIKE A MAN!

BY MARY GODWIN

COVER BY THE Pirate Captain

Note found nailed to Byron's cabin door, pirate boat:

Selfish monster,

Despite my mathematical abilities, I am unable to make the logical connection between my polite messages and the abusive missive found attached to my pillow this morning.

I can accept the comparison to nocturnal animals. They are merely insults. I can bear mockery regarding my prowess at physical sports. I have never seen the purpose of competitive games. But I <u>cannot condone</u> the use of an apostrophe in the word 'turnips'. Are you suggesting that the turnip possesses something? Apparently not – the sentence ends on that very word. Does your Romantic rejection of convention even abhor honest grammar? You claim that words are your craft, but this suggests otherwise. Worse, I strongly suspect you did it deliberately, knowing how such things provoke me.

I cannot share a boat with such grammatical abominations for another day. Thank goodness then that we are taking stage coaches for the remainder of the journey to Ruthven Pass. Any vomiting I do will be caused by my travel sickness rather than poor punctuation.

I should also like to inform you that no part of my anatomy has been 'transformed into turnips' due to neglect. That would be fanciful even by your ludicrous standards.

Charles Babbage

Editorial from **Young, Brooding & Doomed,**
Volume 2, Issue 18, 1816

TIN ✱ BYROBULLETIN ✱ BYROBULLETIN ✱ BYF

A BEDAZZLING BARRAGE OF BARE-FACED BRINE-SOAKED BUCCANEERING!

Ahoy, Byromaniacs!

How is life in the WORLD OF TOMORROW?
Is a TIN BUTLER serving you TEA on the MOON?

'Oh my giddy aunt,' you're thinking, 'Bad Bouncing Byron has finally lost his mind, probably from all the syphilis.' But wait! I can explain. You see, because of the vagaries of the publishing business, I'm writing this <u>several weeks</u> before the issue of <u>Young, Brooding & Doomed</u> that you hold in your excitable hands even hits the magazine stands. And, not only that — there's a good chance your pal is writing to you from BEYOND THE GRAVE! Like a skeleton with a ghostly pencil! I hope I haven't chilled your spines too much with that awful image. Whilst you huddle under a blanket — no doubt reading this in secret, by candlelight, because your mother doesn't approve of my rakish influence on your developing mind, failing as she does to realise that you're a woman now, with a woman's needs — let me explain what causes me to suggest such a ghoulish possibility . . .

As you'll know from my last column, Pulse Pounding Percy Shelley, Marvellous Mary Godwin, and yours truly

have recently embarked upon an adventure with the inimitable
Pirate Captain and his Terrifying Troop of Capricious
Cut-throats. There have been feasts, coffee, poems, tattoos,
trips to the library, cryptic warnings and all sorts of
astonishing goings-on. But now we embark upon the most
dangerous part of our quest — as we journey to Castle
Ruthven, deep in the Carpathian Mountains! What terrible
truths might we uncover there? Who — or what — can have
been responsible for the attempt on the Captain and young
Mary's lives? I have no idea at all. But in the meantime enjoy
this SPOOKY WORDSEARCH. It is designed to
help build up atmosphere.

Excelsior!

Lord Byron

G	H	O	S	T	H	O	U	S	E
U	N	D	E	A	D	P	I	G	S
E	L	D	R	I	T	C	H	I	D
S	C	A	R	Y	G	I	R	L	S
W	E	R	E	J	E	L	L	Y	S
B	I	G	M	O	N	S	T	E	R
G	I	M	L	E	T	E	Y	E	D
S	U	P	E	R	M	O	O	N	S
G	O	T	H	I	C	T	Y	P	E
T	O	B	Y	Y	O	U	N	G	S
S	T	U	P	I	D	F	A	C	E
S	E	A	S	E	R	P	E	N	T

Twelve

DIAL 'S' FOR
SKELETONS

'Is he asleep?' asked Mary.

The Pirate Captain leaned over and poked Babbage. Then he flicked his ear. Then he tugged one of his bushy sideburns. The mathematician let out a little snore.

'Thank Neptune,' said the Captain. 'He wasn't joking when he said he gets travel sick, was he? Doesn't look big enough to hold that much stuff inside him.'[25]

Mary gave Jennifer a gentle nudge. She seemed to be asleep as well. The coach bumped over some rocks, but neither of them stirred. 'I'm glad they've nodded off, Pirate Captain,' said Mary. 'Because I've been looking for a

---

25 Motion sickness is probably caused by the body trying to expel neurotoxins. When the inner ear transmits to the brain that it senses motion, but the eyes tell the brain that everything is still, the brain concludes that it is hallucinating due to the ingestion of poison, and then responds by inducing vomiting to get rid of the non-existent toxin.

chance to talk to you about my novel. The fact is, I've run into a few . . . difficulties.'

'Is it description? I always find that tough.' The Captain chewed his lip thoughtfully. 'The trick is to use all the senses. So, let's say your character was to look out the window of this coach. First off, he'd *see* miles and miles of gloomy forest, plenty of creeping mist, and an occasional glimpse of the moon. He'd *hear* the odd wolf howling and the sound of the other coaches rumbling along the unmade track. He'd *smell* the cedar top notes of his classy aftershave. He'd *feel* a bit uneasy because he's more than a day's travel from the sea and someone once told him that he gets all his powers from seawater. And what's the other sense?'

'Taste.'

'He'd have great taste in clothes, decor and beard styling. Does that help?'

'In a way,' said Mary. 'It's more a problem with the direction that the book's taking. Quite unexpected really. You remember the half-man, half-seaweed mutant? He was supposed to be really vile, cruel, vicious, murderous and so on.

All the other characters feared and hated him in equal measure. Well . . .'

Mary gazed out of the window at miles and miles of gloomy forest.

'Phoebe, the heroine, she's started to see a different side to him. She's developing feelings.'

Mary gave the Pirate Captain a look that he might have interpreted as significant if he hadn't been admiring her delicate wrists and missed it altogether.

'She's not sure whether it's anything serious. They have nothing in common! Phoebe's a progressive woman toiling with the modern world and he . . . he sleeps in a rock pool and survives partly by photosynthesis. But there's something about him. I don't know! A quiet nobility almost. An attractive air of danger. He appears so effortless, whereas Sir Henderson . . .'

'Her betrothed?' said the Pirate Captain.

'Yes. He . . . Well, he seems rather *pedestrian* in comparison. This wasn't how I planned the book at all, Pirate Captain. I don't know what to do.'

'Have you tried having her swoon whenever anybody turns up? That way she doesn't need to do much of anything. I'll let you in on a secret – generally I avoid female characters in my novels because they do different things to men. You can't make a female character set her jaw because the reader just wouldn't believe it. But if I find I've made the mistake of writing a woman into the book, I make her swoon as soon and as often as possible.'

'I don't think you're quite following me, Pirate Captain,' said Mary, slowly, emphasising the words. 'This is the key to her future happiness. Should she stick with Sir Henderson, who, though dependable, doesn't share her interest in experimental vivisection at all, or should she defy society's conventions and hit on the seaweed-man mutant?'

The Captain thought for a moment.

'If she does that, she needs to look out for his beak.'

'Your *beak*?'

'Have you never met a half-man, half-seaweed? They generally have a beak next to their mouth.

Could be a nasty surprise for this Phoebe if she's trying to kiss him and there's a little beak there crying out for fish in a weird raspy voice. "Fiiisshhh! Fiiissshhh!" it'll go. "Giiivvveee meeee fiiiisshhh." That'd put me off kissing for sure.'

'You've lost me, Pirate Captain. Does this represent something profound or do you really have a beak?'

'Me? Not that I know about. But *he* would, wouldn't he? If you want this book to be realistic that is. "Fiiiissssshhh! Fiiiisshhhh!" '

While the Pirate Captain continued to illustrate how the half-man, half-seaweed's beak would talk, Mary sat back and rubbed her temples as if she were very tired. Then, steeling herself, she leaned toward the Pirate Captain once more.

'Captain . . .'

'Last stop!' shouted the coach driver. 'Everybody out!'

'Cogs!' said Babbage, sitting up with a start. 'Oh. Are we here already?'

The pirates, the Romantics and Babbage hefted their luggage off the coaches.[26] Not for the first time the pirate with a scarf wished the Pirate Captain was better at travelling light. He *had* once asked if maybe the Captain didn't need to pack quite so many fancy hats whenever they were away from the boat for longer than an afternoon, but the Captain just responded with a vague excuse about how his physical baggage repre-sented, in some hard to define sort of way, his *emotional baggage*, which was something he didn't want to talk about, and which the pirate with a scarf should be ashamed to have brought up in the first place.

The unlikely group struggled from the mud track towards a village nestling at the foot of the pass. More of the mist hung about doing its thing,

---

26   In the 1860s, California's Wells Fargo posted rules for passengers of their stagecoaches. These included: 'Don't snore loudly while sleeping or use your fellow passenger's shoulder for a pillow; he or she may not understand and friction may result'; 'Forbidden topics of conversation are: stagecoach robberies and Indian uprisings'; and 'If ladies are present, gentlemen are urged to forgo smoking cigars and pipes as the odor of same is repugnant to the gentler sex.'

and a bleak and relentless rain made everything as shiny and slippery as a seal, though not so adorable. Eventually they reached the village's single little tavern, from which spilled the sound of meaningless foreign chatter, and the sort of music that strikes you as interesting when you're on holiday to far-flung climes, but which turns out to be unlistenable in any other context.

'Gracious me!' said Shelley, once they'd got inside and taken off their wet overcoats. He looked about, delighted. 'It's so *authentic!*'

The people crowding the tavern all had the type of face that has its own special section in *Spotlight*. Everybody had the right number of eyes and noses and chins and mouths, but they seemed to have been stuck onto their heads by a particularly cack-handed child.

'We mustn't mention this place to a soul, lest the rest of London society should start to include it on their Grand Tour. It would be overrun by tourists.'

'Aren't we tourists?' asked the albino pirate, confused.

'No, we are *travellers*,' Shelley explained.

'There's a world of difference that I'm not going to go into right now. Mostly it's to do with wearing flip-flops.'

'Hello, characterful local barkeep,' said Byron, waving. 'A flagon of whatever disgusting indigenous drink you probably brew out of wolf skeletons and bits of mud, please.'

'Just look at the man's hands!' Shelley marvelled. The barkeep obligingly held up his hands for closer inspection. 'The stubby fingers of a real culture, untainted by Western values!' He turned to address the entire tavern. 'You know, in many ways all of you strange, hunched-over peasant folk are far richer than us, because you're so much more spiritual.'

The locals murmured a slightly half-hearted 'thank you'. As the Romantics attempted to strike up a conversation about tribal tattoos, Jennifer picked her way across the tavern to where the Pirate Captain had parked himself on a stool. He was pulling wistful faces into his pint glass.

'Hello, Pirate Captain. Mind if I join you?' she said, sitting down next to him. The Captain glanced across the room at Mary and pulled another even more wistful face. Jennifer patted his shoulder. 'You know, Captain, before I joined the crew, all my adventures happened in drawing rooms and on lawns. We didn't have sea monsters or tidal waves so we tried to get our excitement from listening to what people said.'

'Sounds awful,' said the Pirate Captain with a shiver.

'It was,' agreed Jennifer, 'but it taught me something really useful. It's called *reading between the lines*. When people say one thing they often mean something else entirely. The trick is to think about what that could be. So, for example, when Lady Something-or-other talks about an urn in her ornamental garden she's *actually* intimating that the Earl of Wherever is interested in marrying Madame Thingy's niece who was recently in Bath. That's called *subtext*.'

'Subtext?' said the Pirate Captain, blankly. 'Is that like one of Babbage's codes?'

Jennifer nodded. 'That's right. It's like a really annoying code. Here's another example. Imagine a young Englishwoman writing about a nautical mutant. Now imagine she tells a nautical *person* about a plot where a young Englishwoman has feelings for the mutant.'

'That sounds a lot like Mary's book,' the Captain said with a nod. He paused. 'Hang on a tick. I thought you were asleep?'

'I was *trying* to sleep, but you've got quite a loud voice. It penetrates.'

The Pirate Captain took this as a compliment and gave a little bow.

'So I pretended to be asleep rather than get in the way.'

'Do you do that often? Pretend to be asleep, I mean?'

'Don't worry, Captain, I've never noticed you creep into my cabin and try on my clothes at night, and if I had noticed I would be sure to assume it was just the kind of healthy experimentation anybody might do. But you're missing my point about Mary's subtext.'

It took quite a long time for the Captain to really grasp it, even after she'd drawn a few diagrams to help him along.

'So,' said Jennifer, 'to sum up: I think Mary

likes you too. But she's conflicted. The same way you sometimes get conflicted about whether a chop is better than a steak.'

The Captain contemplated. The face the Captain did for contemplating was a lot like the face he did for nodding off, so Jennifer gave him a prod.

'All depends on the context. Is it to go with potatoes?'

'Try to stay on topic, Captain.'

'Sorry. Well then. Mary and me. I think I've got an idea!'

'I suppose it's too much to hope that your idea involves "talking about your feelings like two sensible adults"?'

'It is, sorry. See, if Mary likes this subtext palaver as much as it seems, then it only makes sense for me to use *even more* of my own subtext. It will show we're on the same wavelength. I don't really know what being on the same wavelength means, but I do know that it's one of the most important things to you women.'

'Fair enough,' said Jennifer, who knew when to

cut her losses in a conversation with the Captain. 'So how are you planning to do *your* subtext?'

Before the Captain could reply, Byron's big ringing voice cut right across the noise of the tavern.

'. . . and so that's why we're here to visit Castle Ruthven!' he boomed.

Everything stopped. The barmaids stopped serving drinks. The band stopped playing gypsy versions of popular hits. Even the raven on the roof stopped his atmospheric cawing. A few of the younger pirates thought it was a game of musical statues and so they stopped too, and did their best to freeze in position.

'Did I say something bad?' asked Byron, in as much of a whisper as he could manage.

The barkeep grunted, and reached behind the bar. Then he slapped a piece of paper down on the table in front of the poet. It was a short leaflet printed in English, German, French, Spanish and Japanese.

You've been handed this leaflet because you've expressed a desire to visit Castle Ruthven, seat of the notorious Ruthven counts. Please consider the following points:

- The castle is stricken with a horrifying curse. There are no reports of visitors returning alive.
- Female travellers may want to consider the legend that the last Count Ruthven was said to possess mesmerising powers of seduction that he used to overcome any woman he encountered *even though he wasn't that sexy.*
- He may be immortal, stalk Europe and kill to keep the curious away from a shocking family secret, though this is based on unreliable anecdotal evidence.
- Blood almost certainly drips from the walls.
- There is little plumbing and the rooms are very draughty.

The South-Eastern Romania Tourist Authority recommends travellers visit the new log flume at Carpathian Land or take a fabulous Black Sea cruise with a three-course meal and bingo every night. By accepting this leaflet you are absolving us of any legal responsibility for your impending dreadful deaths.

It was the most bone-chilling tourist information leaflet the pirates had ever read. A few of the crew suddenly remembered they might have left a stove on aboard the boat, and suggested it could be a good idea to go back and check.

Byron, though, just laughed.

'I think you'll find,' he said to the barkeep, 'that we are made of sterner stuff than you suppose. For you see, we travel with the indomitable Pirate Captain! A man who bested the kraken itself! A man who single-handedly wrestled a dinosaur to a standstill in the Bodleian Library! Not the sort of chap to turn tail and run from a horrifying curse. Why, I doubt you'd even find the word "fear" in his dictionary.'

The barkeep shrugged a suit-yourself sort of shrug, and went back to polishing an ashtray.

'He's right, of course,' said the Pirate Captain, nodding to Jennifer. 'If you look in my dictionary you'll find that it goes straight from "fealty" to "feasible". My advice: should Black Bellamy ever turn up on your doorstep offering to sell you a set of reference books, send him packing. His encyclopedias are even worse. It's just the definition of "sucker" repeated on every page for nineteen volumes."

Thirteen

TODAY'S SPECIAL . . .
IS GORE!

If the adventurers had arrived at Castle Ruth-ven two hundred years later they would probably have found it being restored by a bright-eyed young couple with energetic names like Kyle and Marcy. Kyle and Marcy would say stuff along the lines of 'the castle itself is the real project manager' and 'we're simply custodi-ans for the future' and they'd make sure that the new bits looked new, so that you could 'read the continuity of the architecture', and they'd furnish it with some tasteful Eames recliners, and maybe a Barcelona chair, and then they'd sit down in their bespoke kitchen with a bowl of olives resting on the hand-cut Italian tiles and take a moment to gaze proudly at their creation, and then they'd look at each other, and there would be a terrible gaping silence as they real-ised that they hadn't actually got anything in common at all, and Kyle would wonder if Marcy's neck had always been that stringy, and

Marcy would wonder why Kyle still wore those ridiculous distressed jeans like he was a teenager or something and right there and then, they'd decide to have kids, because that at least would give them another distraction to put off the inevitable acknowledgement of the awful, desiccating meaninglessness of it all, but nothing would ever entirely block out that one bottomless silence, and it would loom over them for the next twenty years until Kyle had an unhappy relationship with a local waitress half his age and Marcy ran off to 'find herself' by spending a fortune on yoga and cupcakes and Valium.

But because it was the early part of the nineteenth century all the pirates and their companions found were great heaps of ivy crawling across the crumbling stone walls and an inescapable and unsettling air of dread. The pirates shivered in the moonlight. Obviously it was because they were cold, not because they were frightened of the moon. Stories of dog-eating moon squid were just tales made up to stop young pirates asking for a puppy every single Christmas and birthday. They knew that.

Only Byron seemed immune to the eerie atmosphere, mainly because he was too busy trying to spook Babbage by putting ivy on his head and making Triffid noises.

At the forbidding doorway everybody looked up at the big brass doorknocker. It was shaped like a bat. Next to the door were some gargoyles, which were also shaped like bats.

'Here's an interesting fact about bats,' said the Pirate Captain. 'There's a popular misconception that they're evil creatures who'll go for your jugular soon as look at you. Whereas of course there's actually nothing to worry about, because you're far more likely to get rabies from bat saliva dripping into your mouth whilst you sleep.'[27]

At this point everybody pretended to be really interested in bats for a bit. Once that conversation dried up, they all talked about this weather they'd been having. Then they moved on to anecdotes about the trip so far. But before long

---

27 Another interesting fact about bats: the Honduran white bat has a yellow nose and makes little tents for itself out of big leaves. Aw!

they'd run out of topics and it was obvious that they couldn't really delay the inevitable much longer. The Pirate Captain banged the door-knocker. It echoed a big clanking echo about the mountains. Nobody answered. So, steeling himself, he gave the door a push. It swung open with a creak which, no matter how you tried to spin it, sounded exactly like the noise a pirate or a poet would probably make if they were being crushed under a giant coffin full of severed heads.

'See, where they've gone wrong here is too many cobwebs, rusting suits of armour, and mouldy bits of taxidermy,[28] not enough twigs in bowls,' said the Pirate Captain, stepping into a cavern-ous stone hall. 'Twigs in bowls do wonders to make a house feel more homely.'

'What an abominable place,' whispered

---

28 Before skinning any animal prior to stuffing, have patience – you need to ensure it is cold enough for the blood to coagulate.

Shelley with a shudder, as they wandered from room to room. Everything was damp and dusty, and full of creeping shadows. In some places, where the owner had obviously felt there weren't enough creeping shadows, a few more had been painted directly onto the walls. And where there weren't shadows there were awful portraits.[29]

'Look!' said Mary, raising her lantern. 'These must be all the Count Ruthvens going back through history. Goodness! It doesn't seem like they got much in the way of vitamins.'

The counts were a sickly-looking bunch. One of them had a club foot. One of them had a club foot and a cruel mouth. And one of them had a club foot and a cruel mouth and a face that looked exactly like a cabbage. A few of the pirates pointed and laughed, and said 'cabbage face' until Babbage hushed them with a frown.

'I would rather you didn't jest about the unfortunate fellow,' he said. 'As a man with the

---

29 If you're a newborn chick, you'll crouch in fear at any shadow flying overhead, but very quickly habituate to the shadows of harmless birds like geese and only crouch at the shadows of predatory birds like hawks.

surname "Babbage", and possessing a peculiarly lumpy face myself, it may not surprise you to learn that I have received a fair number of cabbage-based taunts in my time. Please desist.'

'Sorry, Charles, that was insensitive of us,' said Jennifer. 'But you must admit, he really *really* does look like a cabbage.'

'Right then,' said Byron, clapping his hands whilst the pirate with a scarf lit a fire in the castle's study. 'What's the plan? Where do we think this Count might have put "On Feelings"?'

'Well, he's bound to have hidden it some-where ingenious. You wouldn't want to leave something like that just lying about,' said the Pirate Captain, sinking into an armchair by the fireplace and pulling a cigar from his pocket. 'So we need to look for clues. That's the first rule of detectiving: legwork. To that end, I suggest we split up. Mary, why don't you go and check the library? Percy, have a look in the dining room.

Babbage can do the crypt. And Byron can investigate the pantry. Assorted pirate crew, you can look upstairs and check the bedrooms.'

'And what are *you* going to be doing?' asked Shelley.

'Ah well, I've got the hardest job of all,' said the Captain, sitting back and blowing a smoke ring. 'You see, the second rule of detectiving is to *get inside the mind of your suspect.* So whilst you lot are having fun searching everywhere for clues, I'm going to risk life and limb by sitting here in front of the fire, eating a sandwich and imagining what this Count Ruthven fellow might have been like. There's a chance I'll become obsessed and start taking on his characteristics, but that's a risk the criminal profiler has to take.'

Shelley looked a bit unconvinced.

'Also, I can't partake in clue-hunting, because the dust might interfere with my sensitive palate. And where would we be without my famous ability to tell chicken from fish, hmm? Well, come on then, don't just stand there like corpses. Go and find some exciting clues.'

Everybody looked a bit more pale and jumpy when they got back from their clue-hunting, apart from the albino pirate, who just looked a bit more jumpy. Some of the crew had even started to suck on their security blankets, which they knew the Captain didn't approve of, because it failed to strike a genuinely piratical note.

'So, any luck?' asked the Pirate Captain, finishing off some of the port he'd found inside the study's rather gaudy credenza.

'It's horrendous!' said the pirate with gout, miserably. 'There are unexplainable noises and unnerving smells and the curtains taste of fungus.'

'Well, if it makes you feel better, I've had a horrific time too,' said the Captain. 'Look – I spilled some of this port on my best coat. That's not going to wash off in a hurry. So, let's see these clues.'

'I found a clue shaped like most of a dead rat,' said the pirate with bedroom eyes.

'I found a clue shaped like a horrible great pile of cobwebs,' said Babbage.

'I found a clue shaped like an old skull,' said Byron.

'I didn't find a clue,' said Mary. 'But I did find this.'

She hoisted a big glass display case onto the desk. It contained a taxidermy diorama of some stoats playing cards.

'Oh, that's nice,' said Byron. 'I always like a spot of taxidermy.'[30]

'No,' said Mary, pointing at it. 'Look closer.'

When they peered close they could see that actually it was a more gruesome diorama than it first appeared. One of the stoats, who was wearing a little pair of spectacles and carrying a cog, had a knife sticking out of his belly. Another of the stoats, who wore a beard and a tricorn hat,

---

30 If you're mounting a deer's head and want to use the natural skull, remove the eyes, flesh and tongue with a knife and the brain with a long spoon. If you have any problems, boil the head until the flesh turns grey and then remove. Be careful not to boil it too long, as the skull will separate into several parts.

had a miniature noose around his neck. A stoat with a winsome expression was about to drink some poison. The stoat with lipstick was being drowned in a teacup. And the stoat with flouncy hair had a bomb in his lap.

'I think it's another warning,' said the pirate who enjoyed continually stating the obvious. The Captain picked up the stoat that looked a bit like Mary and gave it an affectionate pat. 'Look at that, they've got your lipstick bang on,' he said. 'Isn't that ingenious?'

All the pirates agreed that it was ingenious and more adorable than sinister, so not really worth worrying about. Mary put the diorama back on the floor with a slightly exasperated sigh.

'Anyhow,' said the Pirate Captain, 'that's all any of you managed to find, is it? I mean, I don't want to brag, but see here.' He held up an antique journal. It had the words 'Private! Keep Out!' written across the front. 'I didn't even leave this armchair and I managed to find this stuck down the side of the cushion.'

'What is it?' asked Shelley.

'This Ruthven fellow's old diary. I always enjoy reading other people's diaries.' The Captain opened it and read a page out loud:

13th February 1676: That blue-eyed peasant girl is here milking the goats again. She has a very pretty smile. Think I will get a haircut.

22nd February: Said hello to the peasant girl. She screamed and asked what was wrong with my hair. Mumbled something about wolves. I hate that barber.

23rd February: Spent the afternoon practising my lute near the stables. The peasant girl asked me to stop. She said my playing was very good, but informed me that the goats are allergic to music. She is very knowledgeable for a peasant girl. Not sure she noticed my hat.

2nd March: Asked the peasant girl if she would like to accompany me for a stroll in the woods on her day off, but she said something vague about having to wait in for the plumber. I pointed out that plumbing has yet to reach the Carpathian Mountains. At that point the peasant girl said she thought somebody was calling her from the village. The village is half a mile from here, so I suppose she must have particularly keen hearing.

5th March: Went for my stroll alone. Halfway through I bumped into the peasant girl arm in arm with the stable boy. Asked what had happened to her plumbing appointment, but she just pretended to be a tree.

10th June: Have ceased to think about the peasant girl. I suppose she's attractive in a conventional sort of way, if you go for obvious stuff like a nice figure and tumbling gold tresses, but I have decided that I have more refined tastes.

'There's lots of lovesick nonsense like that,' said the Captain, flipping the page, 'but then it gets interesting:

20th September: Whilst researching the family history, I have made a fantastic discovery! Though I dare not say what, even to you, dear diary. Have booked passage to England. Surprisingly cheap-rate ferry service.

27th September: Not 100 per cent sure about this ferry. Europe to England via Barbados seems like a strange sort of route. Lots more plundering than you would expect.

9th October: The Captain blames 'sea air' for missing valuables and my disordered belongings. Slightly worried that 'sea air' intends to get to Oxford before me. But tomorrow I disembark, and will make utmost haste towards my prize.

The Captain closed the diary. 'Then, after that the entries stop and it just becomes a list of girls' names with marks out of ten. Pages and pages of them.'

'Well, that probably explains how your old mentor wound up with the catalogue number.

But I'm not sure how any of it helps *us*,' said Shelley, folding his arms in a surly way.

'Ah, but that's not all I found,' said the Captain, looking pleased. He held up a piece of antique parchment. 'Because see here – this was tucked into the back of it.'

Shelley took the parchment and studied it for a moment. It was a piece of sheet music with the lyrics to a song. Byron grabbed it from him excitedly.

'Could this be it? Perhaps Plato's treatise is actually a *love song* so powerful it can overcome any lady that should hear it?'

They all gathered round to look at the song.

The Hidden Rules Of Love

'Hmmm. Can't *feel* myself swooning,' said Mary.

'Nope,' said Jennifer. 'Doesn't do anything much for me, either.'

'Must at least be a clue of some sort though?' said the Captain, a little crestfallen. 'Some kind of clever code maybe?'

'How about it, Babs?' said Byron. 'Anything there?'

He passed the piece of music to Babbage, who gave it a cursory once-over, shrugged, and passed it back. 'Not a sausage, so far as I can make out.'

'Damn and blast!' said Byron, scrunching it up and tossing it over his shoulder.

'Well then,' said Babbage, getting to his feet. 'It looks like this entire expedition has been an unfortunate wild goose chase.' He yawned. 'Gentlemen, and ladies, it has been a long day, and the night draws in. I suggest we have little option but to retire to bed for the evening. I for one welcome the chance to spend a night free from clattering hooves or the incessant chatter of weevils.'

A bit reluctantly everybody agreed that Babbage was probably right, so they gathered their things together and went upstairs to choose where to sleep. The Pirate Captain crossed his fingers and hoped that none of the rooms had bunk-beds in them, because he didn't want to have to spend the rest of the night mediating disputes between the crew as to who got to go on top.

A little while later the pirate with a scarf finished his nightly moisturising routine, and headed back towards his bedroom. As he was passing the door to the Captain's room it opened a crack.

'Can I have a word, number two?'

'Of course, Captain,' said the pirate with a scarf. 'Did you want me to brush your teeth for you?'

'Yes, thanks, in a minute. But first, I've got another little job for you.'

He beckoned the pirate with a scarf inside. Then the Captain proudly slapped a bundle of paper into his hands. It was tied together with a bit of twine. 'Ta-da,' he said.

'What's this?' asked the pirate with a scarf, hoping that the answer wouldn't be too stupid.

'Nothing less than a cupid's arrow aimed directly at young Mary's heart!'

The Captain took a moment to get the pirate with a scarf up to speed. He explained all about Mary's secret love of monsters, and about her novel, and about her clever use of subtext.

'So,' he continued. 'I've decided to do some subtext too. To that end I've written an entirely new version of Mary's story, but this time there's none of that conflicted feelings nonsense. In my version the heroine and the monster get it together. Actually they get it together in chapter two, so the rest is pretty racy stuff, as you can imagine.'

The pirate with a scarf flicked through the manuscript. He read a page at random.

Phoebe stepped out of the shower, sensuously towelling off her glistening elbows. Then the wall exploded and the half-man, half-seaweed monster walked in excitingly. 'Hello, doll-face,' said the half-man, half-seaweed monster noisily. 'I have just eaten Sir Henderson.'

'You swine!' said Phoebe breathlessly, first swooning, and then caressing his beak affectionately. 'Oh! But why pretend any more? Let us be frank at last – it is you I have always loved, from the first moment I saw you powerfully wrestle the quarter-bee/ three-quarters-mollusc creature that night in the Limehouse opium den. We should probably elope to someplace hot and get married now. By the way, it is all right if you want to see other women, I'm completely fine with that.'

Then some enemies appeared but the half-man, half-seaweed monster exploded them and ate them too.

'So, what do you think?' asked the Captain.

'I think you like adverbs and unconventional sentence structure,' said the pirate with a scarf, who never really enjoyed these conversations.

'I'm not asking for a *critique*, number two. I learnt a long time ago that writing is a lot like piracy – the trick is to have almost no quality control whatsoever. That's why I was able to knock off an entire novel in an hour. No – my point is, do you think it's *too subtle*?'

'No, Captain, I'll think she'll get the message. It helps that you've included so many graphic illustrations of what they get up to.'

The Captain looked pleased. 'Right then. Here's the plan: first we wait until everyone is asleep, and then, in the dead of night, you'll creep into Mary's room and replace *her* manuscript with *this* one. She'll find it in the morning, read my clever subtext, and bingo! Her little lubber heart will probably swell to twice its normal size. I'm not the sort to count my chickens before they've hatched, but I don't think it's getting ahead of myself to suggest that she'll forget all about Shelley on the spot.' He leaned back on his pillow and went a bit misty-eyed. 'After that I expect our relationship will go through three main stages. At first we'll be totally wrapped up in one another. We'll dance through meadows with garlands in our hair and make daisy chains. I'll make spontaneous romantic gestures and playfully splash her when we're near water. In the next stage, we'll move into a lovely little cottage in the Cotswolds where we'll get married amongst the apple blossom. A simple ceremony, not too many uncles or cousins and we'd prefer to shell out for decent portions rather than table service, so we'll have a buffet. Then we'll have three strapping sons – Chet, Champ and Turlough – and three charming daughters, Marina, Neptunia and Barnacle. In the final stage of the relationship, the children will fly the nest and we'll sit in rocking chairs and think about the old days. She'll have a scrapbooking hobby and I'll grow petunias in the garden because they're hard-wearing. Slugs can be a problem, but apparently you can keep them under control with a saucer of beer half-buried in the soil. Did you know that?'

The pirate with a scarf didn't.

'Our only worry will be Turlough, who'll be more difficult than the other children. He'll make a few bad decisions, but we'll always be there for him, Mary and I.'

'One point I'm not entirely clear on, Captain,' said the pirate with a scarf. 'Why am *I* the one stealing into her room?'

'Well, I'd do it myself, but there's always the risk she'll wake up, which could be difficult to explain. Not the done thing in lubber circles, creeping about a girl's bedchamber. Whereas if she wakes up and sees *you*, we can just inform her that, regrettably, you've a shocking and despicable history of this sort of behaviour.'

So as the grandfather clock in the study chimed midnight, the pirate with a scarf tiptoed across the hallway and into Mary's bedroom. He was relieved to see that she was asleep, snoring loudly, and that right there on the bed next to her was a manuscript. He carefully put the Captain's novel down in its place, and then crept back out again. But he had barely got two steps back towards the Captain's room when he heard footsteps tapping down the corridor towards him. Deciding it was probably best not to be caught red-handed, the pirate with a scarf quickly stuffed Mary's manuscript into the mouth of a shabby polar bear head hanging on the wall. At that moment Percy appeared from round the corner. They both jumped.

'Oh!' exclaimed Shelley. 'Hello. I was just going to get a glass of water.'

'Yes,' said the pirate with a scarf, 'I was also going to get some water.'

'Water is good, isn't it?'

'It is, yes.'

'Well, 'night then.'

' 'Night.'

The pirate with a scarf threw in a bit of innocent whistling for good measure and ducked back inside the Captain's room. The Captain looked up hopefully from his copy of *Barely Human Mermaids*.

'Operation Subtext Switcheroo is a go, sir,' said the pirate with a scarf, doing a thumbs-up.

Fourteen

DEATH PAID
FOR DINNER

The Pirate Captain awoke to the sound of terrible screams, which instantly put him in a bad mood, because in the era before John Humphrys 'terrible screams' was the worst noise you could wake up to. Even bloodthirsty terrors of the High Seas preferred to wake up to birdsong, or someone pretty singing in the shower, or the smell of freshly laundered bacon. He grabbed his dressing gown and tramped blearily out of bed to see what the commotion was about.

In the hallway he found the poets and a big gaggle of pirates all pressed up together by the open door of Jennifer's bedroom.

'What's all the racket, you swabs?' the Captain asked, rubbing sleep goop from his eyes. 'Some of us have spent an uncomfortable night dreaming our beards were haunted by great flapping ghost moths, and would appreciate a bit of peace and quiet.'

Mary waved him over. 'Oh! Captain, it's awful!' she cried. The Captain pressed through the throng and peered inside.

He'd witnessed some pretty shocking scenes in his time as a pirate: a crew of twenty reduced to a crew of three thanks to poor porthole maintenance; a man eaten alive by ants; a menu where half the starters were more expensive than the mains; an ant eaten alive by men; the business with Little Jim; and more besides. But this was worse than all of them. Jennifer was nowhere to be seen. And her bed was covered in blood. Big splotches of sticky bright red blood.

'Moider!' said the pirate from the Bronx, who had been worried that he wasn't going to get a look-in on this adventure.

'I was on my way down to breakfast, when I saw Jennifer's door ajar,' explained Mary. 'So I popped my head in, hoping to have a chat about girl-related matters, and then I found this! What terrible fate do you think could have befallen her?'

The Pirate Captain circled the room, licked a finger and held it up to the air. Then he stroked his beard and narrowed his eyes.

'I'm afraid,' he announced, after a few moments, 'that this looks very much like the work of the ghoulish undead.'

Byron gaped. 'Good Lord! You mean ... a *vampire*? You really think this Count Ruthven chap *does* still stalk these halls?'[31]

The Captain nodded. 'I'm afraid so. Either he's spirited Jennifer off somewhere to be his zombie bride, or he's already sucked the blood right out of her, like she was a flame-haired coconut.' He waved his fist at the ceiling. 'Oh! Why did it have to be Jennifer? There're at least half a dozen members of the crew that I wouldn't even notice if they met a gory end. But Jennifer was different, mostly because she had the full complement of limbs and sensory organs, which is rare amongst seafaring types.'

Byron placed a hand on the Captain's shoulder. 'If it is any consolation, I intend to

---

31 Vampire squids look like they have teeth on the inside of their tentacles and a black 'cape' of webs between them. When threatened, a vampire squid tucks its tentacles under itself to look like a pumpkin. If bitten by a vampire squid, a normal squid does not turn into a vampire squid.

immortalise her in verse.' He stared into the middle distance and pinched the bridge of his nose. 'Oh! Fair Jennifer; with her gentle manner; those sparkling eyes; her bell-like laughter; that ready smile; her full sensuous lips; the firm swell of her bosom; her shapely tapering thighs; that shelf-like . . .'

Everybody listened respectfully to Byron's poem. Once he was done a few of the crew had to excuse themselves to go and take showers. Then everybody gathered in the kitchen for breakfast, because although they were shocked by the latest turn of events, they knew that breakfast was the most important meal of the day, and that it was important not to skip it.

'We should never have come to this place,' said Babbage, looking miserably at his slice of bread. 'I suggest we heed that leaflet's advice and go and conclude this adventure on a log flume.'

Byron thumped the table. 'But we're so close!

I can feel it! Right on the verge of discovering Plato's great secret!'

'What do you think we should do, Percy?' Mary asked, turning to Shelley, who had been very quiet all through the meal.

'Frankly, I don't much care,' said Shelley, sulkily downing his Rice Krispies.

Mary frowned.

'Are you okay?'

'Fine,' said the poet with a cold sort of look. 'Why don't you ask the Captain what our next move should be?' he added, grimacing. 'I'm sure he has some brilliantly improbable stratagem, one that almost certainly involves idiotic costumes.'

Everybody turned to the Captain. He waved a piece of sausage on the end of his fork in a thoughtful way, and smiled.

'As a matter of fact, I do.'

'To catch a dracula, you have to *think* like a dracula,' said the Pirate Captain, after making sure he had established the right atmosphere by

opening and closing the creaky door to the pantry a few times and doing some spooky uplighting on his cheekbones with a candle.

'But how?! How to get inside the head of such a ghoul?' Byron paced up and down, looking even more brooding than usual. 'Would it help to write a verse from the ghastly creature's perspective, do you think? As a sort of psychological exercise? But where to begin? I don't even know what sort of music they like to listen to.'

'No need for any more poetry,' said the Pirate Captain, pulling up a chair and sitting on it backwards, like an olden-days nautical Christine Keeler. 'Luckily, in my years of adventuring, I've had numerous encounters with the spine-chilling, so as a result I'm something of an expert on draculas.'

'An expert to the extent that you still call them "draculas",' pointed out Shelley.

'Draculas, vampyres, fanguloids, gentleman-bats, call them what you will – the point is, they have one fatal flaw.'

Everybody looked at the Captain expectantly. He tapped his nose.

'The common dracula is appallingly vain.'

'Really?' said Mary. 'I didn't know that.'

'Yes, it's sad,' the Captain said, shaking his bushy beard, which almost caught fire on the candle he was using for the spooky uplighting. 'They can barely pass a mirror without preening themselves for hours.'[32]

'I thought they didn't even show up in mirrors?' said the pirate in red. 'Isn't that the whole point of the soulless undead?'

'No, you're thinking of aborigines. The dracula is a narcissistic beast, brimming with an unhealthy self-regard. Just look at the way they dress. And at how our Count Ruthven fellow had this place done out.' The Captain waved at the great hall's sinister decoration. 'The showy interior design of an unchecked ego.'

'It *is* quite vulgar,' said Babbage, looking unhappily at a great big stuffed elk that loomed over one of those medical skeletons.

---

32 Presumably not with 'preen oil'. Vampires' anatomy may be a mystery, but they are unlikely to secrete a waxy oil from a nipple-like protuberance near their tail.

'I like it,' said Byron. 'It's baroque.'

'So what do you suggest we do to take advantage of this singular personality defect?' asked Percy, still looking unconvinced.

'Ah, well – this is the clever bit,' the Captain grinned, and held for one of his famous pregnant pauses. 'We stage a *conference of the macabre.*'

'Conference?'

'Yes! We pretend to hold a conference for all the most horrific monsters in the world. When the dracula realises that he hasn't been invited to our supernatural little gathering, he'll be *outraged.* Especially as it's taking place right here, in his own castle. I'll wager that before we reach item two on the agenda, he'll show himself, unable to contain his wounded pride, and demand in his screechy dracula voice to know the reasons for his exclusion. We, of course, will just lie and say the invitation must have got lost in the post.'

So as dusk fell, it was an odd collection of guests that started to mill about in the ballroom. Anybody paying hardly any attention at all, because maybe they were in a rush and had other more important things to do, might well have agreed that it resembled a gathering of fairly unconvincing creatures, though they'd probably just be saying that so they could get on their way. The Pirate Captain, his beard and face painted a bright and fetching shade of green, stood up behind a lectern and waggled a tentacle constructed from old toilet rolls at everybody.

'Hello, monsters,' he said.

'Hello,' said the monsters.

'I hope you're all enjoying the canapés. Now, I'm just going to go round the room and do a roll-call. The Mummy?'

'Here,' said Shelley, waving about torn-up bits of newspaper that didn't look anything like bandages.

'Generic ghostly presence?'

'Here,' said Babbage from under a large sheet.

'Wolfman?'

'Graaaa!' said Byron, who was wearing one of

the Captain's fur coats and a big papier-mâché wolf's head. Byron was better at making costumes than Shelley or Babbage.

'Mad Axewoman?'

'Here,' said Mary, waving an axe and making her eyes bulge in a mad way.

'Fu Manchu? Gargantua? Man-Eating Plant? Killer Rat? Slime Creature?'

'Here,' chorused various members of the pirate crew.

'And obviously last but not least there's me, the Terror From the Deep. So that's everybody.' He raised his voice. 'Yes, everybody. I certainly can't think of anybody important that we might have left out. Right, so – first order of business. Horror rating. It is proposed that we reduce the horror rating of a dracula to below that of a Giant Maggot. Any objections?'

'Item forty-six,' said the Pirate Captain, stifling a yawn. 'It is further proposed that draculas are only popular with teenage girls because they're regarded as safe, unthreatening boyfriend material.'

'Oh, for pity's sake!' exclaimed Shelley, throwing off his newspaper bandages with a disgusted shrug. 'This is quite useless. Look!'

He pointed out of the window, where the sun was starting to set over the mountains. 'We've wasted an entire day! If you'll excuse me, I've had quite enough of this. I think my time would be better spent writing an angry poem about capricious girls.' And with that he stomped off upstairs. Mary sighed, put down her axe, stopped doing mad bulging eyes and went back to doing regular eyes.

'I'm sorry, Captain,' she said. 'I really don't know what's got into him.'

'Probably belly issues,' said the Captain. 'Whenever I'm in a mood it tends to be belly issues.'

'Shelley does rather have a point,' said Babbage. 'For some unfathomable reason this Monster Conference does not appear to be working. Therefore, I think I might also retire for the night, unless anybody has any other suggestions?'

Some of the pirates had other suggestions, but they were mostly serving suggestions for boiled hams, and so not particularly helpful at that point in time. Byron announced that he was going to be moody in the kitchen. The crew, after a brief vote, all decided to go and spend some more time laughing at the portrait of the man who looked like a cabbage. So once again the Pirate Captain found himself alone with Mary. He tried to do his nonchalant voice, but it came out slightly strangulated.

'So, anyway,' he said, wiping some of the paint off his face. 'How's the novel coming along?'

'Sorry?'

'Phoebe and the, uh, half-man, half-seaweed creature.'

'Oh, well,' said Mary with a little shrug. 'I haven't really had a chance to think about it, what with these terrible goings-on.'

'No, of course, stupid of me.' The Captain tried to hide his disappointment by only cursing very quietly to himself. 'Still, it's important not to abandon your muse. You know, one odd thing I've noticed is that when you reread what you've written after a brief interlude, it often strikes you *entirely differently* to how it did before. So you should definitely take another glance at your manuscript as soon as you can.'

Mary nodded. 'I suppose it might help take my mind off things.'

'No time like the present,' said the Captain, hopefully.

'Yes, Captain, I think I shall return to my room to work on it,' said Mary, getting to her feet and fixing him with an ambiguous stare. 'Perhaps you could walk with me? In case of vampires?'

They stopped outside Mary's room.

'So, here we are,' said the Pirate Captain.

'Yes, Captain, here we are.'

Mary bit her lip. The Captain tugged at his beard ribbons. Wolves howled in the forest outside.

'Anemones are funny creatures, aren't they? Like underwater eyebrows.'

'Anemones?'

'Sorry, I don't know why I said that.'

The Captain stared very hard at his boot buckles and tried to think of some conversation that didn't involve anemones.

'Perhaps,' said Mary, 'you'd like to—'

'*GHOST!*' shouted the albino pirate, as he and the pirate in green came tearing up the stairs, arms flailing wildly. They skidded to a halt, panting and wide-eyed.

'There's a ghost in the study!'

'That's nice,' said the Captain. 'Sorry, Mary – you were saying?'

'A LADY GHOST!' exclaimed the pirate in green.

'Yes, well, good for her,' said the Captain. 'But Mary here is trying to finish her sentence.'

'Why are you mouthing "go away"?' asked the albino pirate.

Down the hall various doors creaked open as the other adventurers poked their heads out.

'What's all the noise?' asked Babbage.

'What was that about "ghosts"?' asked Shelley.

'Did someone say "lady"?' asked Byron.

Fifteen

LOBSTER BOY –
24 INCHES LONG!

Everybody stood in the study looking at exactly no ghosts.

'There was!' insisted the pirate in green, upset. 'A lady ghost.[33] She was ghastly white, but in an attractive way, and she just walked straight through the wall, like – like . . . well, I can't think what like, because I don't know anything apart from ghosts that can walk through walls. I suppose a rhino could walk through a wall, but it wasn't much like a rhino.'

'Also, she was carrying her head under her arm!' added the albino pirate breathlessly, running in a circle. 'And she had three legs!'

The Captain glowered.

'All right, she might not have been carrying

---

33 Byron, when pursued by love-struck Lady Caroline Lamb, described the experience as 'like being haunted by a skeleton'. Prone to melodrama, she once wrote 'Remember Me!' in a book on his desk, which just prompted Byron to write a bitchy poem about her.

her head under her arm and she might have had the regular number of legs,' said the albino pirate, faltering. 'But she really was a ghost. Standing right where you are now. I am sixty-five per cent certain it wasn't my reflection.'

'Sorry,' said the Captain, turning to Babbage and the Romantics. 'Appears to be a false alarm. When the lads get overexcited they have a tendency to start imagining things. I don't like to tell them off for it because I think a healthy imagination should be encouraged and culti-vated, but they do get rather carried away.'

'Well I for one don't think we should dismiss such phenomena quite so readily,' said Shelley, arching an eyebrow and stalking towards the door. 'And, seeing as we are all now up, if everybody would care to join me in the dining room, I believe I have a plan that might resolve our predicament.'

Once they had all taken a seat, Shelley unfolded a square wooden board, and laid it carefully down on the table in front of him.

'That's your plan? We're going to play some sort of *board game*?' said the Captain, frankly unimpressed. 'You think the dracula or his ghostly pal will be so jealous of the thrilling time we're having for ages-four-and-up that he'll pop his head round the door and ask to join in? I know you lubbers have lower standards than us seafaring types when it comes to excitement, but even so, seems far-fetched. Still, nothing ventured nothing gained, I suppose. Where are the pieces? I want to be the thimble.'

'There aren't any pieces, Pirate Captain,' said Shelley, glowering.

'No pieces? Oh, hell's limpets, I've got you – it's one of those role-playing things. In that case, I take my enchanted axe and lop Percy's head off. I think it's your turn next, Mary. Keep an eye out for goblins.'

Shelley groaned. 'This is not any type of game,' he explained. 'It is a Ouija board. A way for us to contact the spirit world.'

'Sorry, I stopped concentrating,' said Byron. 'Caught a glimpse of my cheekbones in that suit of armour. What are we doing again?'

'Desperate times call for desperate actions,' said Shelley. He took a heart-shaped piece of wood from his pocket and placed it on the board. 'Though it pains me to say so, I fear the Captain is correct: obviously some occult forces are at work in this awful place. It is my hope that the spirit world can provide us with some answers, and allow us to uncover the dreadful truth behind Jennifer's disappearance, not to mention the whereabouts of "On Feelings".'

'Oh, what rot,' said Babbage, shifting uncomfortably in his seat. 'This is exactly the sort of nonsense I was expecting from you wiffly types.[34] To think, I could be at home polishing gears and springs.'

'Please sit down, Mister Babbage,' said Percy, suddenly sounding a bit more commanding than usual. 'Now – if you would all link hands, I

---

34 Certain sorts of people like to tell you that 'left brain people' are logical, linear and good at languages while 'right brain people' are creative, open-minded and intuitive. The truth is that all brain functions involve both hemispheres of the brain. Anybody who says this kind of thing is probably stupid, trying to sell you something, or both.

shall attempt to work this device and see if anybody is out there in the spirit aether.'

Everybody linked hands apart from Shelley, who rested his palm on the piece of wood and then half closed his eyes.

'Woooooooooo!' said a ghostly voice.

'Byron, please stop that,' said Percy.

'Sorry,' said Byron.

For a few moments nothing stirred. Then, very slowly, the wooden block under Shelley's palm started to move.

'I think it's working!' whispered Mary, squeezing the Captain's hand.

'Hello?' said Shelley, addressing the shadows. 'Is anybody there? Are you trying to tell us something?'

Eventually the wooden block settled on a letter. It was an 'H'. Then another. E. Then another. L. Then another.

H.E.L.L.

'Great Scot!' exclaimed Byron. 'We've contacted the underworld itself! Oh, I hope it's a succubus. Pretty adventurous girls, those succubi, from what I hear.'

'No – wait! Look . . . it's not finished yet,' said Mary, enthralled. The block moved again.

H.E.L.L.O.

'Ah, that's nice,' said the pirate with a scarf. 'I'm glad the spirit world has manners.'

'Who is this?' asked Percy, his voice trembling.

I.T.S. M.E. J.EN.N.I.F.E.R.

'Jennifer!' exclaimed the Captain. 'Neptune's knees! So you really are dead? We're all very sad. Can you tell us what it's like being a ghost?'

O.K. I. G.U.E.S.S.

'Have you seen anybody famous?'

I. M.E.T. H.E.N.R.Y. T.H.E. E.I.G.H.T.H.

'Is he very fat?'

Q.U.I.T.E. F.A.T. Y.E.S.

Percy cut in over the conversation. 'Jennifer – can you tell us what happened to you?'

M.U.R.D.E.R.E.D!

'By a dracula?' asked Byron, holding his breath.

T.H.A.T.S. R.I.G.H.T.

A chill wind seemed to sweep through the room. The Captain was glad he was wearing his hat, because he wasn't aware that the idea you lose most of your body heat through the top of your head was just a myth.

'What can we do? Where is he? Do you know where he's hidden the missing bit of the book?'

T.H.E. F.I.E.N.D. I.S. . . . .

'Yes?'

. . . I.N. . . . .

'Yes?'

. . . I.N. . . . .

'Don't milk it, Jennifer.'

. . . T.H.I.S. V.E.R.Y. R.O.O.M!

Everybody gasped, and let go of each other's hands.

E.M.P.T.Y. Y.O.U.R. P.O.C.K.E.T.S.

'This is getting idiotic,' said Babbage. 'I will play no further part in such an unscientific charade.'

'You seem very jumpy, Charles – if that *is* your real name,' said the Captain, eyeing the mathematician suspiciously. 'Perhaps you've got something to hide, hmmm?'

'I suggest we do as she says,' said Shelley. 'On the count of three, we all empty our pockets onto the table. Agreed?'

'Because of the ridiculous nowadays fashions, I don't have pockets,' pointed out Mary. 'Will a purse do?'

'I'm sure that'll be fine,' said Shelley. 'Ready?'

One by one they all nodded, even Babbage, though he looked a bit reluctant.

'Right then, here goes. One. Two. Three!'

Everybody thrust their hands into their pockets and plonked the contents onto the table.

'Let's see what we've got then,' said Percy. He indicated the scented handkerchief, squashed lily and well-thumbed thesaurus from his own pockets. 'Nothing incriminating there. What about you, Babbage?'

Babbage mostly had equations written on scrunched-up envelopes, and a few doodles of mechanical ladies saying things like 'Oh Mister Babbage you are a one'.

'Mary?'

Mary just had a notebook and some smelling salts.

'So,' said Percy, turning to the Pirate Captain with a glare. 'How about you, Captain?'

'Well now,' said the Captain, sifting through

quite a big pile of bits and pieces. 'Half a ship's biscuit,[35] my lucky toy unicorn, a novelty astrolabe shaped like a lobster, a selection of drinking straws in different sizes, and the *I-Spy Book of Waves*.'

'Really? That's everything?' Shelley looked a bit disappointed. 'Well, uh, that just leaves you, Byron.'

Everybody looked at Byron. He pursed his lips.

'How odd! Here's a shopping list that I don't remember writing.' He held up a shopping list. It read: *coffin, mothballs for coffin, billowing black cloak, toothpaste*. 'Then there's this petticoat, which looks to be about Jennifer's size, and finally there's this badge that says "I AM A MASSIVE VAMPIRE".'

For a moment, nobody said a thing.

---

35 Ship's biscuits were not in fact infested with weevils as commonly supposed, but with the bread beetle, which is a relative of woodworm. The large white 'maggots' reported in ship's biscuits were actually the larvae of the cadelle beetle. Some speculate that the latter preyed on the larvae of the former and kept those biscuits free from bread beetle infestation.

'Well, would you look at that?' Byron ran a hand through his hair and shook his head in happy disbelief. 'It appears that I've been the evil Count Ruthven all along!'

Sixteen

HAM AND HELLFIRE

'This is fantastic!' said Byron, bouncing up and down. 'Me! The maleficent undead! I've taken "dangerous to know" to a whole new level. The fans are going to be beside themselves when they read about this in the next issue of *Young, Brooding and Doomed*.'

He started to sing a little song to himself about being a vampire. The more easily frightened members of the pirate crew hid behind whatever furniture they could find. The others scratched their heads.

'The evidence does appear irrefutable,' said Babbage, looking sadly at the shopping list. 'And to be honest, I can't say I'm *entirely* surprised.'

'No,' agreed Byron, eagerly. 'I mean the signs were always there, weren't they? Though if I'd had to put money on it I'd have probably guessed I was a protoplasmic nightmare of some description.' He leaned forward and drummed his fingers on the table. 'So, what happens next? Something eldritch, I'd wager?'

'Well, for a start you can tell us what you did to Jennifer, you rogue,' said the Pirate Captain, looking cross. It's hard not to be disappointed when friends turn out to be soul-sucking abominations. 'And then you can tell us where this infernal secret of yours happens to be hidden.'

'Haven't a clue! I don't remember anything about all the stuff I've been getting up to. I don't even know what special powers I've got, though I'm sure they're brilliant. Perhaps I'm only a dracula when I'm asleep? Is that a thing?'

'Aarrrr,' said the Captain, getting up from his chair and pacing up and down the length of the study. 'I think we're going to have to lock you in the pantry whilst we decide what to do with you.'

'Of course, can't be too careful. Don't want me biting your face off.' Byron suddenly threw his head back and bared his teeth with a hiss. Then he grinned again. 'No, see, I'm just messing with you. Right then, in I go.'

Everybody waved as Byron helpfully stepped inside the pantry, and then the Captain and

Babbage made sure the door was properly bolted.

'I didn't really want to say it in front of the chap,' said the Captain, turning to the others, 'but obviously we're going to have to lop his head off.'

'But we can't!' exclaimed Mary. 'I know he's a vampire, but he's still our friend.'

'Yes,' said Percy, shifting uncomfortably from foot to foot. 'I'm sure there's a perfectly innocent explanation for all of this.'

'Sorry, can't risk it. I made that mistake before, when I took on that cannibal boatswain. Remember, number two?'

The pirate with a scarf winced and nodded.

'Kept on assuring me he had it under control, but he'd eaten half the crew before the week was out. It's a shame, because he really did have a lovely singing voice.'

'But how?' asked Babbage. 'How does one kill the awful undead?'

'Well, there're lots of ways,' the Captain explained. 'Lopping his head off is just one of many options. We could set fire to his hair, or stuff a garlic clove in his mouth. Those are the usual methods.'

'No! It's too horrible!' said Mary.

'Fair enough. Well, if none of those grab you, I suppose dousing him in holy water is the most humane/least messy option.'

'And where do you propose that we find holy water?' pointed out Percy. 'Here, in a haunted castle miles from anywhere?'

'Actually, Percy, I've got that covered,' said the Captain. 'A few years back, I got a touch too heavy a dose of tropical sun. I did a lot of things that month, but one of the few that I can remember is insisting I should be allowed to officiate at my own marriage to a turtle. So I took the time to become an ordained member of Black Bellamy's Oceanic Evangelist Church. It's amazing, you just send off your cheque, pick which type of deity you want to worship – I chose that elephant one, with all the arms – and then they send you a certificate through the post. So I'm a fully ordained minister, with legal powers to bestow sainthoods, verify miracles, and, more to the point, bless water. Actually, it doesn't have to be water. I can probably bless a chair. Or a ham. Whatever you fancy, really.'

So, after some surprisingly boring debate about the nature of right and wrong and whether if a vampire bit into a ham it would turn the ham into a hampire or if it would just stay a regular ham, the Captain got the pirate in green to fetch him a big bucket of water from the kitchen. Then he blessed it, which seemed to involve him making a lot of elephant noises whilst doing an odd little dance.

'Okay, everybody ready?' said the Captain, holding up his bucket of water. Mary stifled a sob and nodded. Percy stared at his shoes. Babbage did a thumbs-up and slid the bolt across.

'Count of three. One. Two. *Three.*' With that the Captain kicked open the door and threw the bucket of blessed water as hard as he could into the pantry.

There was a splash. Everybody peeked inside. All they could see was a lot of soggy bread and breakfast cereal. Shelley rubbed his eyes, gobsmacked.

'The fiend has vanished!' exclaimed Babbage, looking about. 'But how?'

The Captain slapped his forehead, groaned, and pointed up to a tiny gap in the wall. 'Neptune's lips! There! He obviously transmogrified into a bat and flew out through that hole. I forgot they can do that.' He sighed, sat down on a stool and ruefully started to chew on a wet bit of Weetabix. 'It's like my old Aunt Joan always used to say: if you're going to end up fighting monsters, Pirate Captain, try to stick to ventriloquist's dummies who have gone alive.'

They spent the rest of the evening searching the castle from top to bottom, but there was no sign of Byron anywhere. Eventually, as the clocks struck eleven, everybody agreed that there was no alternative but to go to bed, and – assuming they didn't all meet a grisly end in the middle of the night – decide what to do in the morning. So reluctantly they tramped back to their rooms, locked their doors, made sure the windows were closed so bats couldn't fly in and tried to get some sleep. Usually the Captain prided himself on being able to fall asleep in any situation at the drop of a hat. Once he'd even managed to nod off in the middle of being squeezed to death by a giant squid. But now he found he couldn't get comfortable. He tossed and turned and every time he *did* get close to drifting off, he'd suddenly hear a noise. He tried to console himself with the thought that a nervier pirate would think the creaking sound was a wooden ghost opening its mouth ready to gobble him up. Or that the hideous shuffling from outside his door was an awful headless horse about to strangle him with its terrible hooves.

Tap! Tap! Tap!

The Captain let out a shriek.

'Pirate Captain?' whispered the headless horse from outside the door. It was quite well-spoken for an unnatural monster that presumably spoke through a severed windpipe.

The Pirate Captain shrieked again, but this time with as much dignity as he could muster. If he was going to get eaten alive by a headless horse then he planned on doing it with aplomb.

'Captain?' repeated the headless horse, now sounding uncannily like Mary Shelley.

He opened the door a crack and peered out. Sure enough, Mary stood there wearing a long white nightgown and some sort of complicated woman's sleeping bonnet that framed her face in a particularly attractive way.

'Hello, Mary.'

'Were you shrieking?'

'Yes, just practising my girlish shrieks. I'm entering an improbable competition of some sort.'

He did another shriek to illustrate.

'Anyhow, what are you doing shuffling about like a headless horse at this time of night?' he asked. 'Not really safe with Byron on the prowl.'

'Oh, Captain, I can't sleep. Can I come in?'

'Of course. I was sleeping like a baby, by the way, aside from the shrieking.'

'I can't stop thinking about my novel,' said Mary, perching on the end of his bed. The Captain noticed now that she was clutching the manuscript to her breast. 'I'm starting to fear it's cursed. That my love of monsters has somehow beset us with this *actual* monster. Do you believe that possible? Could one's own imagination call forth a corporeal horror?'

'Oh no, that almost never happens. I spent ten months marooned on an island trying to will a ham shrub into existence, but with no joy.' The Captain paused, and tried to do a casual face. 'So, your novel . . . how is it? Any interesting bits leap out at you?'

'It's useless,' sighed Mary, 'and I am nowhere nearer to finishing it.'

'You're not? Are you *sure*? Can I have a look?'

Mary passed him the manuscript. He flicked through it. To the Captain's bafflement it seemed that it hadn't changed at all. Everything was still written in her looping handwriting, and there was none of his clever new subtext or slightly obscene illustrations to be seen anywhere.

'This doesn't make any sense,' said the Captain, frowning.

'You've spotted a plot hole?'

'No it's just . . . the pirate with a scarf is usually so reliable.'

'Pardon?'

'Sorry, nothing. Just thinking out loud.'

'To be honest, Captain, I'm considering abandoning the whole thing,' Mary sighed again. 'Because I have reached something of an impasse. There's a scene I simply don't know how to write.'

'Oh dear. Anything I can help with? You've tried my capital letters trick?'

'It's near the end. Phoebe still doesn't know her own mind. She's torn. So she goes to the sea monster's cave lair. She fears he will try to seduce her. Or rather, she is not sure if she fears it . . . or hopes for it.'

She gazed up at him expectantly. It struck the Captain that it was just possible Mary was doing her subtext thing again. But he wasn't entirely sure. If Jennifer hadn't got herself eaten by a vampire then she might have been able to help him out at this point. People, he reflected, could be selfish.

'If he *was* to seduce her, how do you think it might go, Pirate Captain?'

The Captain pondered. 'Well, I have a feeling that the half-man, half-seaweed mutant would skirt about the issue rather than come straight out with it. "Would you like to rub the gas-filled bladders on my ventral surfaces?" is too blunt. The art of seduction is about saying less with your mouth than with your expressions, gestures and undulating, swaying movements.'

'Go on,' said Mary, trembling a bit.

'Their eyes would meet. Not literally, that would be disgusting. More like this.'

The Pirate Captain gave Mary a meaningful look.

'Oh, you monster!' said Mary. 'You knew I'd come tonight! You know I can't resist your soulful eyes, both your normal eye *and* the compound eye . . . panted Phoebe.'

No going back now, thought the Pirate Captain. He took off his hat.

'What do you expect? You've bounced a rainbow off my heart, dear Phoebe. Just your name is poetry to my ears. For these past weeks I've been unable to think of anything else. I've lost so much, but all I can think about is your smooth face and sensuous lips . . . breathed the half-man, half-seaweed mutant.'

Mary bit her lip again. 'You heathen brute. Every fibre of my being tells me to flee, but my quivering femininity, and this waterlogged wetsuit, keep me rooted to the spot!'

There was a pause.

'Said Phoebe,' added the Pirate Captain.

'Of course,' said Mary.

There was another pause, this time with added metaphorical sparks flying.

'Captain,' said Mary.

'Yes?' said the Captain.

'I . . .' Mary looked him right in the eye. 'I think . . .'

And at that moment the pirate in green and the albino pirate burst in through the door, wide-eyed and gasping.

'GHOSTS!' they cried.

'Oh, for the love of kelp,' said the Pirate Captain.

'I don't know if you remember Aesop's fable about "the pirates who cried ghosts",' said the Captain, as the albino pirate dragged him by his sleeve out of his bedroom and down the stairs, 'but I seem to recall that they stopped crying ghosts because an angry pirate captain had run them through in a particularly vicious manner.'

'It's definitely ghosts this time. Possibly more than one. Listen! It's coming from the crypt!'

When they reached the door to the crypt, the usual crowd had assembled. They all strained to listen. There were undeniably ghostly noises emanating from within. Strange rustling sounds, and the occasional terrible moan.

'That was definitely a ghostly wail!'

'And that bump sounded exactly like a head being chopped off!'

'Though I can barely credit such a thing, it does seem like some fearful occult gathering is taking place,' muttered Babbage.

'All right,' said the Captain, rolling up his sleeves in a resigned sort of way. 'But this is the last sinister door I'm going to go through on this adventure. Three is my absolute limit.'

He picked up a lantern, pulled open the door, drew his cutlass, and crept inside the crypt.[36] The rest gingerly followed him in. Picking their way past big stone tombs, the little group advanced towards the awful ghostly sounds. Something moved in the corner. The Captain raised the lantern to see what was going on.

'Kraken's eyeballs!' exclaimed the Pirate Captain, at the grim spectacle that confronted him. For there, stretched out on a sarcophagus, lay the pale lifeless body of Jennifer, and looming over her, apparently just getting ready to take a big bite out of her neck, was Byron.

---

36 The Royal Navy stopped using cutlasses for boarding actions in 1936. The US Navy used them until 1949, the year the Soviets exploded their first atomic device.

Seventeen

THE INTESTINE
THAT CAME BACK

'Hello, Pirate Captain,' said Jennifer's lifeless body, sitting up and adjusting its blouse. 'You really ought to knock, you know. It's very impolite to just go barging in to crypts like this.'

'An apparition! And the beast himself, no less!' cried Babbage, trying to curl up into a ball. The Pirate Captain leaned forward and gave Jennifer a poke with his cutlass.

'You smell nice, for a ghost,' he remarked.

'I'm not a ghost.'

'She isn't,' agreed Byron.

'Well, a zombie corpse then.' The Captain waggled his cutlass at Byron. 'And don't you get any closer, you monster.'

'I haven't been murdered,' persisted Jennifer, 'and Byron here isn't a vampire.'

'But we've caught him red-handed,' said Babbage, 'about to drain the blood from your semi-clad body!'

'He wasn't about to do any such thing.'

'Then what *was* he doing?'

Byron fought back a grin. Jennifer arched an eyebrow. 'Well,' she said, 'sometimes when an attractive man and a free-spirited girl find themselves with time on their hands, things take their natural course.'

The pirate crew went on doing their blank expressions.

'Oh, good grief,' said Jennifer. 'Do I need to draw you a picture?'

A few of the pirates asked for a picture. Some of the more naive ones contended that this still didn't explain the ghostly wailing sounds. The pirate in green seemed ready to cry.

'Come on, you lot,' said Jennifer, hopping down off the sarcophagus. 'It's a bit nippy in here, so let's all go and light a fire in the study and I'll explain everything over a nice hot mug of tea.'

'Right, has everybody got a drink?' Jennifer asked. 'I have a feeling that this is going to turn into quite a long explanation, so we don't want anybody getting thirsty.'

'If you'll allow me, Jennifer,' said the Pirate Captain, brandishing a pipe he had produced from somewhere, 'I think I've already solved the mystery, using my famous nautical powers of deduction.' He turned and eyeballed the assembled little group. 'That's right, ladies and gentlemen of the jury, because if Byron isn't the dracula, then it can mean only one thing. The actual dracula is *someone else entirely*.' He held for a dramatic pause, then wheeled around and pointed an accusing finger at the pirate in red. 'Villain!'

The pirate in red groaned, and slapped his head with a seal flipper.

'No, Captain, it's not the pirate in red. And there isn't any sort of dracula. Let's begin at the beginning, shall we?' Jennifer leaned against the mantelpiece and started to explain. 'You see, that first night when we all went off to bed, I couldn't get to sleep. I kept thinking I heard an ominous eerie rumbling. But I quickly realised that the rumbling was my belly, and that I was just really hungry. So I went downstairs to the pantry to get some toast and jam. It's quite cold in this castle, so I took the toast back upstairs to bed with me. Only then I managed to get jam all over the bed sheets. I don't know why you all assumed it was blood. If you'd looked closely you'd have seen pips, which blood doesn't tend to have.'

'This is why I'm always telling you coves not to eat snacks in your hammocks,' said the Captain to the pirates. 'It's unsanitary. No wonder we've got so many rats knocking about the boat.'

'So anyhow,' continued Jennifer, 'I went *back* downstairs looking for a cloth to wipe it up. But then I heard a sound coming from the library. Curious, I tiptoed inside to see what was going on. The last thing I remembered was some great big owl flapping at me, and then bang! it bopped me on the head. A little while later I woke up, confused and disorientated, inside the crypt of all places. The door was bolted, and I didn't have a clue what to do. But luckily I stumbled upon a *secret passage*. It turns out this place is riddled with them. Since then I've been walking about, trying to find my way out, but it's like an impossible dusty maze. I did find my way out for just a moment, when I believe the albino pirate and the pirate in green saw me – a bit covered in cobwebs – but I think I was still rather concussed, because I managed to get turned about and wandered straight back into the secret passage again.[37] After an age it spat me out in the pantry, where I encountered Mister Byron. He told me he was a vampire and that you were all about to dispatch him in a grisly fashion. He felt that might be for the best, but I didn't think it sounded like a very good idea at all, so I took him off into the secret passage before you had the chance to do anything daft. Eventually we found our way right back to where I'd begun, in the crypt. Well, by that point I'd had my fill of wandering about secret passages, so Byron and I decided to find some other ways to occupy ourselves. And then of course, that's when you lot turned up.'

37 Spiders' webs are rich in vitamin K, although you'd have to eat loads to get your recommended adult daily intake of 120 micrograms a day.

'So who was it that bopped you on the head and trapped you in the crypt?' asked the pirate with a scarf, who was good at identifying the pertinent questions to ask.

'A mystery!' exclaimed the Captain, tapping his temple. 'But not so great a mystery that it can withstand the detective genius of the Pirate Captain. The clue was in that last confused glimpse you caught of your assailant. Fair enough to think you were being attacked by an owl, because it was dark and you were getting bopped on the head and you're a lady, prone to overwrought flights of fancy. But it was no owl. It was a person *with a face a bit like an owl*. Because you, Charles Babbage,' the Captain whirled around and did his finger-pointing thing again, 'are a dracula!'

'I am no such thing,' spluttered Babbage.

'We'll see about that!' said the Captain, quickly blessing his tea and then throwing it over the mathematician. For some reason he didn't burst into flames. He just dripped a bit.

'Oh good grief,' said Babbage, wiping his spectacles. 'Look, I confess – it *was* me that bopped Jennifer on the head.'

'But why?' the poets gasped in unison.

'Well, there's no point in hiding it any longer. The truth is, I wanted "On Feelings" for myself.'

'You old dog!' boomed Byron. 'I didn't know you had it in you. Bad news though, Chuck, I don't think they had mechanical ladies in Plato's day.'

'No, it's not quite like that.' Babbage tried to dab himself dry with some napkins. 'I have, as you know, been working for some twenty years now on my difference engine. A computational device of enormous power. One that can alter the face of society.'

'Go on,' said the Captain, tugging his lapels in the way he'd seen lawyers sometimes do.

'For these past millennia, human relationships have been left in the idiot hands of capricious fate. But my machine could change all that! An opportunity to finally match lonely hearts together on the basis of sensible criteria. It is my contention that people do not necessarily know what is good for them. A pneumatic young lady may *think* she wants an athletic, rippling-torsoed type. Whereas, in actual fact, she might be more suited to a more nebbishy intellectual sort. Well, through the use of punch cards my difference engine is able to work out exactly who is compatible with whom, thereby taking the ridiculous palaver of romance from the equation. Completely removes the need for fruitless chit-chat. But if the contents of this infernal book should be made public then that's my entire business model down the drain. A disaster!'

'Still doesn't explain bopping poor Jennifer on the head.'

'The song! I mean, a child could have worked it out. The musical notes! Look at them.' Babbage took the scrunched-up sheet of music from his pocket.

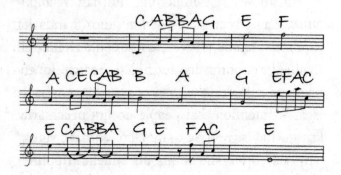

'See? "C", "A", "B", "B", "A", "G", "E", "F", "A", "C", "E". Cabbage Face!'

'The portrait of the man with a face like a cabbage!' exclaimed the pirate who liked to spell things out for those who were slow on the uptake.

'Exactly! Plato's missing treatise was obviously hidden behind the painting. I came down that first night to retrieve it after everybody had gone to bed. But no sooner had I got my hands on the accursed thing than I was interrupted! Somebody was coming! I was quite terrified, so I hid behind the door, and then, in a panic, I bopped them on the head. Obviously I felt terrible when I saw it was Jennifer. I would like to take the opportunity to apologise.'

'That's okay,' said Jennifer. 'No harm done.'

'Well, I was in a fluster. I couldn't think what to do. So I dragged her to the crypt and locked her in, intending to concoct some excuse and explain myself to the lady later. But when I returned to the library, the treatise – which I had rather foolishly left on the table in plain sight – had vanished! As, to my dismay, had Jennifer, when I went back to the crypt later that night.'

'So you mean . . . somebody *else* made off with "On Feelings"?'

'Yes, and I have a suspicion as to who. Because when I was returning to my room, I caught a glimpse of another person up that night, creeping along the hallway . . .' Babbage took his turn to do his own bit of pointing. 'It was Shelley! Shelley took the book!'

'A-ha!' said the Captain. 'Just as I expected all along – the dracula is Percy!'

He threw some more holy tea at Shelley, who also failed to go on fire.

'You've all got it quite wrong,' said Shelley, glowering at his ruined shirt. 'Yes, it's true, I was up that night. But it wasn't because of this confounded "On Feelings". It was because of Mary. I am not so blind that I can't see when a fellow is hitting on my fiancée. I had my misgivings from the start, which is why I slipped from the boat and followed you to the library in Oxford. Where, I'm afraid to say, whilst attempting to eavesdrop I rather clumsily managed to knock an entire bookcase over. Then, later in the tavern, I overheard the Captain and Jennifer talking about Mary's manuscript.' Shelley cast a reproachful eye towards Mary. 'I didn't even know you were writing a book! Anyway, I was worried about this subtext Jennifer claimed to have spied, so I waited until everybody had retired for the night and then crept into Mary's room whilst she slept. I grabbed the manuscript from beside her and took it to my own room to see for myself.'

'But . . . you can't have done!' said Mary.

'I did. And what I found horrified me to my core. For a start, the subtext was all too apparent. You had chosen the Captain over me! But worse, so much worse, was just how bad a writer you are,' Shelley shuddered. 'I mean, really, really awful.'

'No, but I mean, you *can't* have taken my manuscript. I still have it. Look . . .' Mary darted out of the room for a moment and then came back a minute later with her manuscript in her hand. She dropped it on the table. 'See?'

Shelley looked baffled. He pulled another manuscript from his trousers. 'Then what on earth is this?'

'So let me get this straight,' said the Captain, who was starting to get a bit of a headache. 'Byron isn't a dracula. Babbage isn't a dracula. Percy isn't a dracula. Who does that leave? Mary? It's okay if you are, I'm sure we can find a way to make it work.' He threw some more of the tea at her. 'Sorry, that was a reflex.'

'NOBODY IS A DRACULA!' said Percy with a shriek. He sat down and took a few deep breaths to get his composure back. 'I staged the seance to frame the Pirate Captain as a woman-murdering vampire because I thought that would put Mary off him. But I got in a muddle, because Byron was still wearing the Captain's coat from the imbecilic monster conference, so I inadvertently planted the evidence in the wrong pockets.'

'Well if it wasn't you, who *did* take "On Feelings" after Babbage found it?' asked Byron. For a moment nobody spoke. Then Mary sighed.

'It was me,' she said, wiping some tea off her face.

'Why would you do such a thing?' asked Shelley, his turn to be perplexed.

274

'Because it sounds terrible! Romance shouldn't be based on secrets and trickery! Good grief, you might as well go back to hitting us over the head with clubs. Relationships should be about delicate moments and the thrill of uncertainty. It's only any fun if there's a good chance the other person is going to hate you. That's why I painted the warning on the side of the boat in Oxford, but of course nobody took a blind bit of notice.'

'Was the taxidermy you too?'[38]

'Yes. Well, not the whole thing, obviously. I just customised a pre-existing diorama that I found in one of the bedrooms.'

'It was very good,' said the Captain. 'I like the way you used pipe cleaners for the nooses.'

'Thank you. Where was I? Oh yes. So I crept downstairs to search for "On Feelings" while everyone slept. And there it was! Just sitting on the desk where Babbage must have left it. I didn't care how the book got there, I just grabbed

38 Don't be afraid to ask your friends and family for constructive criticism of your finished taxidermy. You can only improve by listening to honest opinion.

it and ran straight back to my room, intending to destroy it. Only before I had a chance, I saw a shadow outside my door! Well, I did the smart thing and pretended to be asleep. But whoever it was crept straight in and snatched "On Feelings" from the bed! And then, I think, replaced it with something else. What was especially odd was that a second later someone came in AGAIN, and took back whatever it was they'd put there in the first place.'

'Well, I'm lost,' said Byron.

'Me too,' said Babbage.

'Yes, and me,' said Percy.

'I think I can explain,' said the pirate with a scarf, looking a bit sheepish. 'You see, the Captain here asked me to swap Mary's novel for his own, somewhat more forthright version.'

'What on earth for?' asked Mary.

'Subtext. Long story. It seemed to make sense at the time,' said the Captain.

'Anyhow,' the pirate with a scarf continued. 'Obviously what happened is that I must have picked up "On Feelings" thinking that it was Mary's manuscript. Easy mistake to make. One lot of papery stuff held together with string looks a lot like the next lot of papery stuff held together with string. Then I left the Captain's version in its place.'

'So the manuscript I stole wasn't Mary's, it was the Captain's!' exclaimed Shelley, relieved. 'Which of course explains why it was so terrible!'

The Captain scowled. 'Yes, whatever.' He turned to the pirate with a scarf. 'So, here's the million doubloon question, number two: what did you do with what you *thought* was Mary's manuscript?'

The pirate with a scarf shrugged. 'I hid it in the polar bear's mouth.'

There was a pause.

The Pirate Captain looked at Mary.

Shelley looked at Mary.

The Pirate Captain and Shelley looked at each other.

And then they both leapt from their seats and raced out the door.

'$*@£!£$ hellfire,' said Mary.

Eighteen

KISSED BY RAT LIPS

Much has been written about Percy Bysshe Shelley. He is described as 'consecrating the profound wisdom of poetry' and 'spontaneously and faithfully embodying the spirit of both intellectual and political revolution'. But nowhere is it said that he could run faster than a pirate captain trying to get to a stuffed polar bear's head. As it happens, he *could* run slightly faster, but the Pirate Captain had a head start so they arrived at the top of the stairs at the same time.

Both of them plunged their arms elbow deep into the creature's mouth, like a pair of reverse James Herriots. After rooting around for a few moments it was Shelley who finally pulled a sheaf of yellowing paper from the ursine maw.

'Ha-ha!' He let out a triumphant cry, but the Captain grabbed the other end of the bundle and gave it a sharp yank.

'I'm terribly sorry,' said the Captain. 'But I

think it's probably better if I take this, for safe keeping. Stop it falling into the wrong hands.'

Percy grunted, tugged back and tried to pull the Captain's beard off for good measure. 'I must apologise too, but I think it's better *I* keep hold of it, lest some unscrupulous hirsute character should try to use the contents for untoward purposes.'

The Captain trod on Shelley's toe, which had the desired effect of making the poet yelp and let go of the manuscript. But before the Captain could pick it up, Shelley spun about, yanked at the polar bear head with as much strength as he could muster – about 30psi – and prised it from the wall. There was a popping noise as he plonked the bear's head down on top of the Captain's head as hard as he could.

'Ooofff!' said the Pirate Captain, momentarily blinded. He tripped, reached out to break his fall, and tumbled straight on top of his pale adversary. They wrestled about on the carpet. If they had been naked and if the Captain didn't have a polar bear head stuck on his face it would have been just like the bit in *Women in Love*.

Peering out from the bear's mouth, the Pirate Captain managed to head-butt Shelley with his snout and grab the sheaf of papers back again. He clambered to his feet and started to run across the landing, but Shelley made a last desperate lunge for his ankles. The Pirate Captain lost his footing once more, and as he reached out to brace his fall, 'On Feelings' went looping off into the air. Shelley gasped and grabbed for it, but only succeeded in knocking the Captain sideways, sending both of them tumbling down the staircase. They landed in a sprawling heap at the bottom, just as the others emerged into the hall. 'On Feelings' fluttered down a few inches away. The two men dived on top of it.

'Give it here, you nautical buffoon!' said Shelley.

'Go suck a barnacle,' said the Captain.

Babbage scowled, and turned to Mary. 'You know, young lady, you could probably save us all a lot of bother if you just *chose* one of them.'

The Captain and Percy paused their tug of war and looked up. Mary bit her lip.

'But how?' she said, sounding plaintive. 'It's an impossible choice!' She slumped into a chair and rubbed her temple. 'I don't know what to do. There's Percy, dear Percy, who really is incredibly smart and refined and has lovely slender hands . . .'

Percy waved the hand that wasn't holding 'On Feelings'. Everybody agreed that they were pretty nice, sort of delicate without being actual girl's hands. Mary smiled at him. 'He even seems to like me having opinions, which is pretty rare in an age when "being a woman with an opinion" is the best way to get banged up in an asylum. But then there's the Pirate Captain. He's more like a force of nature. Like . . . like being hit in the face by the Atlantic Ocean.'

'See?' said the Pirate Captain, shooting his crew a look. 'Notice that she didn't mention whelks? She had every opportunity.'

'He's invigorating and he likes monsters and his hands are rough and manly and sometimes *that's* what a girl wants.'

'Hmmm. I can see your dilemma,' said Babbage, who was starting to enjoy this, because he thought maybe the situation could be modelled with game theory.

'You know, I often encounter a similar problem. Perhaps I can help?' said the Captain, holding up his free hand. 'When I wake up in the morning, I face a tricky conundrum: do I have my egg poached or boiled? You know where you are with a poached egg. It's all there in front of you, perhaps a little showy and patronising at times, but dependable. Sits nicely on the toast. It's not going to run off with a cocktail waitress, is it?'

Everyone agreed that poached eggs were a valid breakfast choice.

'But sometimes I like to walk on the wild side. I want my morning egg to give me a little rush of adrenalin. That's when I go for boiled. The thing about boiled eggs, Mary, is that you never know what's inside. Was it done properly? Will the yolk run or is it solid? Maybe there's a little dead chick in it? Who can say? Only the boiled egg has that element of danger. It's into you, but it would be the first to admit that it's not very consistent or good at commitment. Sure, we both know that egg will be a rollercoaster ride of an egg, but think of the *adventures*.'

The Pirate Captain summoned up another dashing grin.

'In case you missed that subtext, I'll also chuck in a free pair of pirate trousers and you can have number two's telescope.'

Even at the best of times Percy's posture wasn't exactly brilliant, but now he sagged like a limp daffodil. He let go of 'On Feelings' and buried his face in his hands.

'Oh, what's the point? I can't compete with that.' He sniffed, wiped his eyes, and managed a rueful smile. 'To be honest, it's almost a relief.'

'A relief?' said Mary, looking puzzled.

'I'm not an *idiot*. I know full well that some-one like me couldn't hang on to a girl like you. I mean, I do my best. I spout all this flouncy nonsense to try to keep you impressed, but deep down, I knew it would never be enough.'

'Hang on,' said Mary. 'What do you mean, "flouncy nonsense to keep me impressed"?'

'The sensitive brow business. Constantly banging on about Orpheus. Good grief, do you have any idea how *irritating* it is to hear yourself using expressions like "youth's starlight smile" all the time?'

'Oh *Percy*. What made you think I was into that kind of thing?'

Percy shrugged. 'I just thought it was what you girls liked. Though now I realise that it seems I should have been more like the Captain here. This is a man that's true to himself. He must be, because I don't think anybody would act like that by choice. Go with him, Mary. I hope you'll be very happy with each other.'

And with that, Shelley began to blubber uncontrollably.

'Well now,' said the Captain. 'That's worked out well, hasn't it? The best pirate won and all that.' He gave Shelley a pat on the head and clambered to his feet. 'So – now to see what old Plato had up his sleeve, hmmm?'

The Captain licked a briny finger and started to turn the first page of 'On Feelings', but Mary grabbed his wrist and looked deep into his eyes.

'Captain, I implore you. This godforsaken book is too dangerous. Look at what it's turned us all into! Monsters! Not the good kind of monsters with webbed feet and vestigial tails, but the awful metaphorical kind of monsters, which are much worse and much more dull. Please, Captain, there are some secrets we're simply not meant to know.'

'But we've had an entire adventure just trying to find it. Seems pretty ridiculous to stop at this point.'

'If you have any real feelings for me, Captain,' said Mary earnestly, 'you'll destroy this book once and for all.'

The Captain paused. He looked at Mary's nice hair, then he looked at 'On Feelings' sitting on his lap, then he looked at Shelley, then he looked at Byron, then he looked at Jennifer, then he looked at the pirates, then he looked away because the albino pirate was chewing with his mouth open. And then he felt something that had only troubled him two times before, one of which he had mistaken for indigestion. He had a moral dilemma.

The Captain set his jaw, and strode back into the study. The others rushed after him. They found him paused by the fireplace. A long moment ticked by. And then he threw the sheaf of paper straight into the flames.

'What on earth have you done?' said Byron, covering his eyes in dismay.

'Oh, Captain! Thank you!' said Mary, running over and giving him a hug.

The Pirate Captain gazed at where the horizon would have been if there'd been a horizon in the study, and looked as noble as you can look when you have a polar bear's head stuck over your own head. 'Sometimes,' he said, 'a pirate must weigh the responsibility of his actions. He must put aside his own desires and see the bigger picture. He must reach deep inside, and become a better man. Oh, I was tempted. To learn those secrets! To be a god amongst men! To banish irritating will-they-won't-they situations for ever! But I have performed this selfless act for you, Mary, and for the good of civilisation itself.'

He finished and everybody clapped. There wasn't a dry eye in the room, apart from the eyes on paintings. Even Babbage dabbed a tear from his cheek.

Then the Pirate Captain did a bow. It would have gone down in history as one of the Captain's better speeches right up until the bow, but at that point 'On Feelings' dropped out from under his coat and plopped onto the carpet, slightly undermining the whole effect.

'Arrr,' said the Captain, looking down at it awkwardly. 'How did that get there?'

'Pirate Captain!' exclaimed Mary.

'Now, hang on a tick.' The Captain started to back away. 'I realise this must *look* a lot like I did the old switcheroo move again, and that I must have just now swapped "On Feelings" for the copy of your novel that you'd left sitting on the table, which I then burnt in its place, but actually this can be explained. By yet more ghosts. Or some other, much less implausible excuse than that.'

Mary slapped him very hard on his muzzle. Babbage and Byron both eyed the bundle of paper on the floor and subtly started to edge towards it.

'Oh for pity's sake,' said Jennifer. She marched across the room, picked up 'On Feelings' and threw it into the fireplace. 'Good riddance!'

Everybody gasped again, but not very hard because they were getting quite tired now. The Pirate Captain hefted another great sigh, watched the pages crackle and curl into a black ash, and not for the first time wished he had actually been a sexy fireman.

Nineteen

THE ABHORRENT
ALBATROSS

The pirate boat bobbed about in the sparkling Neopolitan bay as everybody gathered on deck to say their goodbyes. They'd spent most of their journey back from Romania retelling their adventure to each other over various feasts. Byron's account of events had gradually grown more and more fanciful, until by the time they reached the shores of Italy he was convinced he actually had turned out to be a vampire after all, and nobody really liked to correct him. Mary and Shelley had passed the time having long conversations about things that genuinely interested them. Babbage was travel sick. And the pirate crew had clanked happily about in some of the suits of armour that they'd stolen from the castle.

'Is that the lot?' the Captain asked, as he helped lug the last of the poets' suitcases down the gangplank.

'I believe so,' said Shelley, awkwardly extending his hand. He squinted in the sunlight. 'So. No hard feelings? When I started this adventure I must confess to not really trusting you piratical sorts, but it seems to me now that you're all right.[39] And I can hardly blame you for fancying Mary. Only a fool *wouldn't* fancy her.'

The Captain grinned. 'Yes, no hard feelings, Percy. I'm not the kind to bear a grudge. Mostly because I'll have forgotten this whole adventure by next week.' He tapped his head. 'The long-term memory is pretty shot, you see. It's from drinking too much seawater.' He took Shelley's hand and gave it a friendly shake. Then the Captain turned to where Byron, now sporting some glued-on fangs and a thick velvet cloak despite the balmy weather, was giving Jennifer a hearty embrace.

'Byron, it's been a real pleasure.'

'Likewise!' boomed Byron.

'Anything exciting planned next?'

---

39 Shelley's body washed up in Italy in 1822, possibly murdered by pirates.

'I thought Jennifer and I could go and have a series of spin-off adventures where we solve occult crimes in far-flung locales. But, alas, she has turned me down.'

'Sorry, Byron,' said Jennifer. 'It's tempting, and you really do have lovely cheekbones, but I can't give up being a pirate. It's just the sort of girl I am.'

'So what *will* you do, Mister Byron?' asked the pirate with a scarf.

Byron tapped his nose. 'Well, my fall-back plan is to sleep with women in a variety of specific locations across Europe, so that if you plot them on a map it spells out BYRON . . .'

'That's quite—'

'Wait, I haven't finished: so it spells out BYRON HAS SLEPT WITH WOMEN IN ALL THESE PLACES. Then I might go off and find a war to fight in.'

'And how about you, Babbage?' asked the Captain.

Babbage was back to looking like the happier kind of owl. 'This adventure has finally convinced me that the heart is too unknowable for mathematical quantification, Captain. However, with

Byron's help I have formulated a new purpose for my machine.' His voice dropped to a whisper. 'You see, through the attachment of a simple mechanical arm, some chalk and a blackboard, I believe it will be possible for my difference engine to draw pictures of ladies in a state of near undress, in homes across the land. Indeed, I now foresee this as being the primary use for my invention for centuries to come.'

The Captain shook his hand as well. 'Well, good luck with that. It sounds like a very admirable goal.'

Mary was the last to head down the gangplank. She and the Captain hovered for a moment, both trying to think what to say.

'So you've definitely chosen Shelley then?' said the Captain eventually, puffing out his cheeks. 'Not too late to change your mind. Swap your pencil for a cutlass. I'd let you play with the astrolabe. It's surprisingly fun.'

'I'm sorry, Pirate Captain – my mind's made up. Now Percy's dropped the pretentious act, I can talk to him about monsters and he can talk to me about things besides poetry.' Mary gently took his hand. 'You're lovely, but . . . well, you're just not great boyfriend material. The fact is, you have absolutely no self-control whatsoever.'

'Fair point,' agreed the Captain. 'Between you and me I'm no good at sharing either. Comes from growing up with a lot of brothers. Or being an only child. I can't remember which. Anyhow, sorry about the business with the book, and burning your novel. In retrospect that seems quite rude.'

Mary smiled. 'Don't worry. As it happens Percy has encouraged me to start a brand-new one. It's quite high concept.'

'Ooh. What's it about?'

'There's this sinister Doctor Frankenstein and he makes a monster out of people bits.'

'Sounds good,' the Captain said, nodding approvingly. 'A "Frankenstein" is a *great* name for a monster.'

'No, Captain, you're not really listening again, the—'

'The Frankenstein Who Walks Like a Man Because of His Man Legs! GRAAA! I'm a Frankenstein!' The Captain mimed being a monster made out of people bits.

'Frankenstein smash!'

'Goodbye, Captain.' Mary gave him a kiss on his hairy cheek. Then she turned and, without looking back, walked down onto the dockside.

Later that night, as the boat sailed through the calm Tyrrhenian Sea, the pirate with a scarf found the Captain sitting on the shoulder of the figurehead, gazing up at the sky.

'Hello, Captain.'

'Hello, number two.'

'Are you okay?'

'Aarrr. Yes. Fine.'

'That felt like a very successful adventure to me, sir.'

'Of course, shame I forgot to bill them after all that.'

'Don't worry, Captain, something else will come up. It usually does. Anyway, I think you've taken the whole Mary thing very well.'

The Captain sighed. 'Oh, well. You know. It's not like it could ever really have worked out between us. I mean, can you imagine what the Pirate King would have said if I brought a lubber home to Skull Island for Christmas? It would have been a scandal.'

He leaned back, lit a cigar, and blew one of his smoke rings.

'Still, it's nice to think that somewhere out there,' the Captain gestured vaguely at the great blanket of stars glittering above them, 'maybe there really is a Phoebe and a half-seaweed, half-man mutant. And perhaps they're sitting arm in arm on some strange alien beach and she's stroking the gas-filled bladders on his ventral surfaces, and he's brushing a curl of hair out of her face. Do you think that's likely, number two?'

The pirate with a scarf didn't really know anything about the probabilities of other worlds containing alien life, or about the idea that maybe there were an infinity of universes all nestling on top of each other, so he just shrugged. 'I don't see why not,' he said.

And with that, the pirate boat sailed about some more.

Appendix – On Feelings

INT. SAUNA. ATHENS – DAY

Socrates enters and sees the young athlete Protagoras.

SOCRATES: Hello, Protagoras!

PROTAGORAS: Hello, Socrates.

SOCRATES: You seem far from your usual carefree self.

PROTAGORAS: Wise, observant Socrates! This is so.

SOCRATES: Here, let me give you a back rub.

PROTAGORAS: Thank you, Socrates.

SOCRATES: Gosh, I can really feel the tension in your shoulders.

PROTAGORAS: I am beset by worry.

SOCRATES: Is it the coming games? You need not be anxious! You throw that discus like

Zeus himself. I've watched you practise. It's quite a spectacle.

PROTAGORAS: It is true, the training progresses well.

SOCRATES: Anyone can tell you've really been working out just from looking at you. These biceps are like rocks.

PROTAGORAS: Thank you, Socrates.

Protagoras loosens his toga and stretches.

PROTAGORAS: No, it is not the world of sport but affairs of the heart that hang heavy with me.

SOCRATES: Sorry, what? I got a bit distracted just then.

PROTAGORAS: Perhaps you might help me, kind Socrates. You are familiar with the mysteries of women?

SOCRATES: Oh. Yes. Obviously. Good old women. Can't get enough of them.

PROTAGORAS: There is a young Spartan maiden whose eye I wish to catch, but she seems oblivious to my very existence.

SOCRATES: Ah.

PROTAGORAS: I have tried wearing an interesting hat, but to no avail.

SOCRATES: Well then, young, fresh Protagoras, I suppose I must tell you.

PROTAGORAS: There is a solution to my problem?

SOCRATES: There is. Listen close though, for it is a secret only a few of the most noble born Athenians are privy to. The key to the human heart itself. Are you sure you wish to know?

PROTAGORAS: Tell me! Oh tell me please! I would do anything to know such things.

SOCRATES: You cannot unlearn this knowledge. It will change your world. Are you *sure*?

PROTAGORAS: I beg you, Socrates!

SOCRATES: In order to win the heart of the one you love, you must remember this.

Socrates pauses, and does a drum roll on an urn.

SOCRATES: First you must cultivate an air of General Disinterest. Then you must demonstrate Great Wit. And finally you must appear

305

Distractedly Philosophical. It never fails, because it's foolproof. Though, if it *should* fail, a further stage would be to pretend that you had a terminal illness.